THE DEAD IN THEIR MASSES

Corpse Fauna
Volume Three

JAMES CHAMBERS

BRAM STOKER AWARD-WINNING AUTHOR

THE DEAD IN THEIR MASSES

NEOPARADOXA
PENNSVILLE, NJ

PUBLISHED BY
NeoParadoxa
a division of eSpec Books LLC
Danielle McPhail,
Publisher
PO Box 242,
Pennsville, New Jersey 08070
www.especbooks.com

ISBN: 978-1-949691-07-8

An earlier version of *The Dead in Their Masses* were previously published as "The Dead in Their Masses," *The Dead Walk Again*, Vince Sneed, ed., Padwolf Publishing, 2007.

All persons, places, and events in this book are fictitious and any resemblance to actual persons, places, or events is purely coincidental.

Copy Editor: Greg Schauer
Interior Design: Danielle McPhail,
Sidhe na Daire Multimedia
www.sidhenadaire.com

Cover Art: Glen Ostrander
Interior Art: Jason Whitley
Cover Design: Mike McPhail,
McP Digital Graphics

FOR BILL, WHO REHEARSED
SO ENTHUSIASTICALLY
FOR THE ZOMBIE MOVIE THAT NEVER WAS.

CONTENTS

Whitley 2019

THE DEAD IN THEIR MASSES

ONE

Turned out Lohatchie was a long way off, and the road there a hard bastard with a chip on its shoulder. It got rough the second we broke out of Warden Lane Grove's prison, but even so, none of us would've ever willingly gone back inside. Della, Mason, and I took the only way left open to us: out into the dark and dying world. So we fought past the living dead things that came for us. We beat them back, and we cut them down, and we left them lying broken in the mud and grass. And we ran. Until stitches of pain laced our sides and we panted for breath, we ran. And when the crowds of the dead that crammed against the prison walls thinned out and fell behind us, we pushed ourselves harder still, stopping to fight only when the wormfeeders came too close or swarmed us too deep to go around them. We crossed the wooded hills by sparse moonlight, chipping away step by step at the twelve-mile stretch between the prison and Mason's house. We fled from hundreds of the dead, put down three dozen or more, and took our fair share of scrapes and bruises along the way. Mason got the worst of it when he slipped down a hill onto a pile of deadfall that gouged a six-inch gash in his leg. Della dressed it tight with a handkerchief, and we kept moving. The dead lurked everywhere, and the night seemed endless—but at least we were free. That thought kept me moving all night until, in the hour before dawn, we reached Mason's house.

We approached the back door through a yard overgrown with neglected grass and tangled weeds. A child's play set shone dully in the morning twilight. On the edge of a half-finished patio stood a barbecue grill draped in canvas spotted with bird droppings. Behind it lay a pile of bricks beside a rusty wheelbarrow. It all seemed so ordinary, so quiet except for the moans of the wormfeeders carrying through the air. But for a blessed moment, there wasn't a dead thing anywhere in sight, so we seized the chance to scramble into the house unobserved.

After we locked up tight and covered the windows, Mason lived up to the promise he'd made before we left and fed us. We ate only canned food and powdered drinks made with bottled water, but my first meal as a free man since I'd been arrested and gone inside tasted like a feast. Later, our bellies full, we took turns showering while the sun came up. Afterward, Mason gave me some of his old clothes to change into so I could shuck my orange prison suit. He let Della pick what she wanted from his wife's wardrobe. Then we slept for twelve hours straight and awoke after dark.

Only we three out of the group that had planned the prison break made it out alive. Before the dead plague, Della had been a nurse in the prison infirmary and Mason a guard. They'd known each other since high school, not friends exactly, but a hell of lot better than either of them knew me. I'd only been on the inside for few months—one of them spent in solitary—when the dead began to rise and the world went to shit. I wondered how they felt having to put their trust in a bank robber, a killer, and now, I suppose, a fugitive too. Not that anyone remained to hunt me down. And anyone who tried would have to make their way past all the living dead folks roaming around outside, same as we did. The same as we'd have to do all over again when we set out for my place in Lohatchie.

Mason's house offered us food and comfort, sure, but not safety.

The dead filled his street and more kept coming from the east, from the direction of the prison, where thousands of them remained only a few hours walk away. They'd seen us pass by in the night and come looking for us. They sensed us hiding—fresh, live meat for them to sniff out like pigs rooting for truffles. They searched for us with cloudy, dead eyes and the incongruously bright eyes that gazed out from the wrinkled slits on the backs of their hands, on their necks and shoulders, and their chests and legs where clothes had rotted away. Those terrifying and inexplicable eyes where none should be. None of us understood them or what they meant, but the dead didn't care what we thought. They simply stalked the block, waiting for some sign of our hiding spot, and though we made sure not to give ourselves away, the longer we stayed at Mason's the more likely our luck would run out like luck always did.

If we'd stuck to my plan, we would've packed Mason's car with food and gear that night and gone on our way the next morning before more of the dead moved into the neighborhood. But right around midnight Mason collapsed. One minute he stood by the picture window, spying through the blinds at half a dozen wormfeeders struggling along the street, and the next, he staggered, gasped, and then folded to the floor. I lifted him onto the couch so Della could tend to him. He burned fiery with fever, and sweat soaked his clothes. We undressed him. The skin around the bloody furrow in his leg flared crimson and pus crusted the wound. Infection had set in, and Mason had bled much more than we realized. I knew then it'd be a while before we went anywhere.

Fortunately for Mason, Della was a damn good nurse, and she had brought along a variety of antibiotics, which she fed to Mason and made sure he swallowed. It still took three days of care to get him back on his feet. We spent most of that time in the living room, Mason on the couch, each of us afraid to leave his side, to leave each other alone. While Della nursed him, I saw the sparks of a deeper bond forming between them, and I figured that no matter how much I helped them, no matter how long we stuck together or how close the three of us might get in the coming days, the time would come when I'd be the odd man out.

I came from a different place than Mason and Della, and it didn't matter that the entire world had fallen into chaos. Except for the dead not staying that way, the rules of nature hadn't changed. Like would still gravitate to like. On one hand, Mason, rugged and all-star handsome, a man with a clean record, a gentle touch, and a fearless light burning in his eyes, and on the other hand, me—a smartass killer wanted in nine states before the FBI locked me up. The kind of man Della had spent her life despising, the kind Mason had worked to keep behind bars. I had become the savior they were counting on to guide them to a safe home, but once I'd done that—maybe they'd turn on me, maybe not. But they'd never consider me one of them.

That's all it took for there to be *us* and *them.*

I tried to put it out of my mind while we waited for Mason to heal.

I felt sorry for him, suffering in a house full of reminders of what he'd lost in the dead plague. Framed photos of his family. A spilled basket of Transformers figures and Hot Wheels cars. Women's magazines left open on the kitchen table, never picked up again. Della told me about the last time Mason had seen his family alive: They'd come to the prison, his wife and two boys, with a busload of refugees begging protection behind the walls. Not only did that son of a bitch Grove turn them away, claiming it was God's will they were on the outside when the dead plague began, but he ordered his guards to fire on them. His idea of mercy. The ones who died got up and killed the rest. And Grove made Mason watch.

That marked the real difference between me and Mason.

He'd bought into the game, played by the rules, and worked hard for everything he had, but when it mattered most the rules of the game changed and stole all the things he valued. Pretty much how it always goes when you're dealing with authority. Those with power may treat you right when times are good and they're feeling generous, but they never let too much slack in your leash. They like to keep you close and controlled. I'd never given a damn for all that happy good citizen bullshit. What Mason lost had been taken from him. Everything I'd ever had, I'd taken for myself, and when I lost it all, I lost it myself too. I got Evelyn and our unborn child killed during the last bank job we pulled. I shot the bank manager who killed her to death, along with the two guards backing him up. Then I ate a life sentence like a sap because I thought I didn't deserve any better. But I'd left all that back inside the prison walls and made my peace with it. I wanted my freedom again, and that's why Della and Mason would never fully trust me. We simply didn't play by the same rules.

Understanding that got me thinking more than once while Mason healed and the dead gathered around us that I should take the car and light out on my own. I couldn't do it, though. Even if some day down the line they did toss me away like garbage, I couldn't leave Della and Mason trapped to die; I could be driven to kill but I wasn't a killer by nature. I only hoped Mason would heal fast so we could be on our way before it became impossible to drive a car down the street.

As it turned out, we cut it damn close. The same day Mason finally got back up on his feet long enough to move around, a couple of wormfeeders camped out in his yard. Their rotting, hungry faces stared at the front door like they saw right through it. Eyes on their foreheads and cheeks, on their arms and abdomens watched and waited. Three more arrived by twilight, another four before midnight, zeroing in on us, and we noticed then how they seemed to be hardening, their flesh turning leathery, the spread of rot arrested, as if they were toughening up, hardening into some final form, another mystery none of us knew how to explain. That night we packed the car, a black Toyota Camry with nearly a full tank of gas, in Mason's attached garage and prepared for our trip to Lohatchie, to my cabin there in the Everglades, far and away from anything like civilization or what little remained of it, a place so isolated we hoped we might be able live in peace there.

The next morning, we hit the road.

TWO

The dead chased us down the street. They flooded out from the yards and houses, forming a gray wedge of walking decay that clamored after us as Mason floored it to the corner, cut the wheel, and sent us barreling down the road toward town. Under different circumstances, the sight of those dumb corpses stumbling and tripping over each other as they shrank into the distance behind us might have been comical, but I didn't feel much like laughing. We'd cut it a lot closer than I'd liked.

Another day—hell, even a few more hours—and the dead would've been too dense to drive past without slowing down and fighting our way through them, and how the world worked now, speed and motion equaled life, while death waited for the slow or timid.

Mason's car held up well despite the beating it took from bad roads and sudden impacts with occasional wormfeeders too clumsy to get out of the way. As we drove out of town with the roar of the engine thundering in the quiet, I thought about how we were running down the new American dream: living long enough to reach a three-room swamp shack where no one would ever come knocking, hoping we could live there free from the smothering crush of the dead, and maybe when we died, not get back up again. After our first day of driving, though, I got the idea the road itself was dead set against us. Things worsened the closer we drove toward town, but they didn't get horrendous until we tried to take the highway. All six lanes, north and south, resembled a scrap yard patrolled by the dead instead of junk-yard dogs. I'd expected it to be bad, but when Mason stopped the car at the top of the entrance ramp, more than a hundred wormfeeders turned and stared at us from the rows of immobile cars, their attention drawn by our presence. As far as I could see in both directions along the highway, more of the dead wandered. The stench coming off the road made me nauseous. I rolled up the window as Mason threw the car into reverse and guided us toward the back roads, the only ones left passable.

Houses and stores rolled by, and Mason asked me, "How long did you figure the drive would take?"

"North Carolina to South Florida? About fifteen hours driving straight through, so I figured two or three days things being what they are," I said. "But I sure as hell didn't count on that."

Della leaned between us from the back seat. "Better accept it's going to be a long trip, boys."

"Shit." The word left my lips on a long breath.

Della proved right. It got no easier as we headed south. The longer we traveled broken roads populated only by the rotting dead, the more I felt like a helpless pariah trapped between a killing field and an infinite and hating sky. The total absence of aerial clutter and mechanical noise—of any human life other than our own—hammered home our utter isolation. I've always considered myself a loner, except where Evelyn was concerned, but even I felt like we no longer belonged in this world. The new world cast us as aberrations, throwbacks with no place left for us.

Still, we drove, even when we could only go in circles until a path forward became clear, but no road we traveled was ever really clean of the dead. A few here and there often turned into a hungry mob with an insatiable appetite for living flesh when we drove too slow or idled too long. That fear kept us moving even on those bone-weary nights when we all wanted to curl up in our fatigue and sleep all the way through the next day. Instead, we took turns napping in the car and stopped only during daylight to scrounge for supplies, food, and fuel, wherever we could find them. We were warm-blooded ghosts haunting an abandoned maze choked with ruined vehicles and burnt-out ghost towns populated by hordes of the dead. They forced us to double back almost every day, sometimes more than once, sometimes a hundred miles or more, to find another way south. We lost days at a time.

A week passed, and we hadn't reached Florida yet. Della became a sullen shadow lurking in the back seat. She did her share of the driving and rooted around for supplies when we stopped, but she kept her distance from me and Mason and seemed jumpy much of the time. Mostly she said nothing nonessential. I credited the change in her to fear and depression, but I didn't understand the edge to it, not until on one of those backtracking detours, Della opened up about what had really been on her mind.

"You know, before all this crap with the dead, I was married and divorced twice?" she said.

Mason and I eyed her, surprised, unsure of her point.

"That's right. Both those bastards beat on me and cheated on me, and I put the second one in a coma with a crowbar the last time he came at me with a belt in his and anger in his eyes. Even holier-than-thou Warden Grove made a pass at me in that damn prison. So I've been riding here this whole time wondering which one of you was going to come at me first to demand a pound of flesh, and neither of you has so much as laid a finger on me or given me a sideways look, and just now, I mean right then when we made the turn, I started wondering if it was *me.* Am I not your type? Am I losing my looks? How damn crazy is that?" She laughed and covered her mouth with the back of her hand. "You two just aren't like that, are you? Like so many other men. Now I actually hope we might live through this, which I didn't back at the prison. I prayed then that every single one of you crazy fools pushing each other around, playing power games, and mind-fucking each other would be wiped off the earth with the damned wormfeeders. You two have treated me well enough, though, so I suppose all is not lost. There's still some light left in the world. We shall go on somehow."

Mason and I took that as a compliment. In fact, we started laughing so hard at the idea that the two of us had restored Della's faith in the future of humanity that Mason pulled the car over. All three of us got out by the side of the road and gasped for air until the uproar died down to a chuckle. Before then, it had never crossed my mind that there might be more to Della than what she showed on her surface. She saw the humor in what she'd said as clear as we did, and for the first time I felt the three of us all really moving together in the same direction, and I felt pretty good about it. Felt almost like the old days of me and Evelyn blazing a trail of robbery from state to state, making headlines, and scribing a big "fuck you" to the law.

Miles further down the road, though, embraced in the quiet that often chases such moments, I thought about Della's time trapped in the prison after the dead began to walk, one of three women among hundreds of convicts. Maybe Warden Grove had lived up to his high ideals, warped as they were, and protected her and the other ladies stuck inside with us. But even if he had, he couldn't have shielded Della every hour of every day. The weight of that sank into me and deepened my appreciation for Della's toughness. She'd lost as much as me or Mason, and she was a survivor. I decided then that if she wound up with Mason, if that's what she wanted, I'd do nothing to stand in their way. Not that I relished the idea of winding up on my own, but I wanted to repay her trust. And when it came right down to it, I was no stranger to being alone.

THREE

A day later, finally across the Florida state line, we pulled into a gas station in some pisswater town where the post office and the firehouse shared a building—a day's drive off our route seeking a way around a worm feeder-infested rest stop on the main highway. The town looked empty of the dead as well as the living, but like I said, no town ever gets really free of the wormfeeders. While Della and I worked the gas pumps, Mason broke into a police cruiser parked outside the garage. He checked the trunk for guns and gear but found the remains of a legless, hungry corpse.

The legless thing hoisted itself on its hands and lunged onto Mason. It dripped a trail of ripe intestines and tacky viscera, while its liver dropped out the bottom of its torso like a black, bloated egg. The dead thing dug its cracked teeth into Mason's cheek and bit down. Mason yelled for help and started shooting. Five rounds punched craters of putrid flesh and blood out the thing's back, but it held on tight.

Mason hopped around and tried to shake it free while Della and I ran to help. Della tugged on the corpse by the ragged end of its filthy shirt, but the cloth tore away in her hands. I planted my shotgun between Mason's chest and the wormfeeder's neck and fired. Mason howled at the noise and concussion, though none of the shot hit him. The dead body broke apart and fell to the concrete. It flopped around on flapping arms, launching gobs of bloody sludge from the stump of its neck. The head held on tight, though, way too close to Mason for me to risk another shot from the scattergun. Instead I pounded on it with the stock, hoping to rupture it like a pumpkin. A patch of bone the size of coffee can lid cracked loose and pin-wheeled away, exposing a dark slick of rotten gray matter.

That's when an eye popped open in the folds of the thing's brain and glared at me past the jagged edges of its busted skull. Pure white with an iris the color of sand. An eye where none should be. It blinked from between folds of necrotic brain tissue, watching me the way a wounded fox might watch a wolf. Its gaze crawled over me, made me queasy; the stare of those damned eyes was the most repulsive thing I'd ever experienced. I drew my automatic and poked the barrel into its pupil. Then I pushed the head away from Mason and fired. The skull burst in a splash of black and red.

Mason screamed. He swatted and clawed at the viscous blowback splattered onto his face, wiping away chunks of bone and meat. He dropped to his hands and knees and heaved until his stomach hit empty. Then he fell over on his back, chest pumping as he caught his breath. Blood dribbled from his wounded cheek. Della knelt beside him to treat the bleeding with a clean cloth from her kit; she sanitized the wound and then packed it with gauze. Bad as it looked, it wasn't deep, and it sure didn't dampen Mason's spirit. He shouted some downright nasty phrases whenever Della's nursing stung.

I picked up a stick lying in the grass and used it to sift through the quivering remnants of the head. The largest chunk of brain splatter on the pavement shimmied and then sprouted another cold eye, a twin of the one I'd shot. Its gaze hit me like a cold breath and left me feeling kind of sick and poisoned. I drove the tip of the stick into the pupil, burst it, and then flicked the whole mess into the tall weeds beyond the edge of the parking lot.

Della's screams snapped me back.

Things shouldn't have happened how they did then, but strained past our breaking points and worn down from running day and night, we didn't realize the toll it had taken on us or how badly the sight of those awful, dead eyes rattled us.

No excuses, though. We got sloppy.

It was too late before I turned around.

We'd forgotten to destroy the torso. It crept up beside Della and shoved her aside. Its cracked ribcage leaked a tail of dead organs as the thing clamped flylike onto Mason and drove one of its splintery hands into his chest. The corpse dug in deep, ripping cords of flesh and cracking ribs as it excavated Mason's heart and raised it toward a phantom head. It acted on the instinct to feed even though feeding was now impossible for it. My eyes fixed on Mason's living heart, crimson and fat, pumping uselessly in the wormfeeder's gray, rotten fingers. It glistened in the morning sun and washed the concrete with its steaming blood. Mason screamed until his voice died with him.

I gathered Della and her kit and rushed us back to the car. A wormfeeder appeared across the street, a group of them down the block, all headed our way. No point staying. Nothing we could do for Mason, and we had enough gas to carry us for a good while. But we had to get clear fast. Seemed obvious to me it was the right move, but that didn't stop Della from swearing me up and down and calling me a coward or from punching me hard enough to leave bruises. I weathered her storm until we made it outside of town, and then, afraid to lose control of the car, I pulled over on the grassy shoulder. Wormfeeders stood a couple hundred yards down the road, moving slow but eyeing us. They headed our way the second the car stopped.

Della jumped out and slammed the door.

Give her a few minutes, let her work it out, I thought.

I hoped she'd see things how they'd been, otherwise, this hard patch could get tricky fast. If she harbored some illusion that we could've saved Mason after his heart had been torn out—that I'd dragged her away, left him to die when we could've helped him— it would put a fine crack between us, and she might wind up wondering if I might run off on her to save my own skin. I massaged the aches in my bruised arm and waited out her rage, keeping an eye on the dead down the road as they drifted closer.

Della shook as she sobbed. I watched her in the rearview mirror, one hand planted on the trunk holding herself up, her tangled, black hair draping her face. She spun around, screamed some more, kicked something in the road, then after a little while, she rubbed her tears away on the back of her hand and got back in the car. The stark redness in her eyes frightened me.

"I'm sorry," she said.

"Yeah. Me too."

"We both know that didn't have to happen."

"No, it didn't," I said. "We fucked up. We let Mason down, and now he's gone, and I feel like hell about it. At the end of the day, he was nothing but good to us. But it ain't gonna do us any better to break down. I'm not saying we shouldn't mourn him. He was our friend and a good one. But let's take this experience as an object lesson about letting circumstances get the best of us."

Della looked wired, ready to fly off the handle again, to go on working out her anger by hitting me some more, but instead she sucked down a few deep breaths and settled into her seat.

"You're right," she said. "There are wormfeeders up the road. Let's get out of here. Fast."

"You got it."

I let out a little sigh of relief. Then I gunned the engine and we drove in silence.

The road rolled away beneath our wheels, and a harsh sun marked our passage.

Couple miles later, Della said, "Shit, Cornell, we have to go back and burn him. I can't stand the idea of him becoming a wormfeeder."

"No can do. We go back, we'll wind up dead like Mason, and all three of us will rise," I said. "All that commotion and spilled blood probably pricked up the senses of every hungry corpse for five miles. Besides it's not Mason getting up, only his body. Mason's dead and gone now and free of all this bullshit."

Della sniffled. "You think that's true? You think our souls go free when we die?"

I hadn't exactly said that so I didn't answer. I'd never wondered much if souls even existed let alone what happened to them after death. Figured everyone learns that when their time comes, so why waste effort on idle speculation? Better to live in the moment, do what you needed to get by. But whatever the truth, I didn't want to believe there could be any human part left in the nightmares that plagued us.

"I'm gonna miss him," Della said.

"Me too," I told her.

Neither of us mentioned Mason again for several days. The wound needed time to scab over. I tried to find meaning in Mason's death, but there wasn't any. He had been a good man. He should've had a better life and a better death, but then these days what *should be* and what *is* were like a pair of bitter ex-lovers. Cold as it may seem to think of such things after losing a good friend, I knew from the moment Della got back in the car that she and I were going to wind up much closer than we ever would've if Mason had lived. It didn't feel right to me then but I knew it would be okay later. Maybe if I'd saved Mason nothing would've ever flared up between us. That would've been all right, I suppose. Least then we might've avoided that lonely detour into some of the worst business I've ever witnessed among the living or the dead.

So much for learning our lesson.

FOUR

My fear of losing Della tripped us up.

Time was I had a good woman at my side and not a shred of doubt in my heart, back when the world was still a place for the living. Evelyn had been one of a kind, and in no way did Della a substitute for a past love. Had Evelyn lived, with my child growing inside her, maybe we would've married, maybe even gone straight before we were caught. Who knows? My life would've followed one different path or another—but I might never have become the kind of man who could survive in a world overrun by the dead. Or maybe I'd always been that kind. I don't know. I'd made my peace with Evelyn's ghost the night we broke out of prison, so she and I were square as far as I was concerned. Aside from a passing resemblance in the right light, Della and Evelyn had little in common, and what I felt for Della was a different thing altogether than what I'd felt for Evelyn.

I'd never once felt an urge to shelter Evelyn from the violence and danger around us. Hell, half the time she was the one looking out for me on a job. Our relationship was a true marriage of equals. With Della, we were equals in another way, but something in her character made me want to shield her. Not that she needed it. She was smart, tough, and dangerous when she had to be, but that didn't change how I felt. It didn't help that Della went along with it to humor me, I guess, or maybe because she liked to have a protector or because it helped her feel a little bit normal again to be playing boy meets girl like in the old days before the dead plague.

Whatever the explanation, that feeling is why I made her wait in the car while I raided the police station in a godforsaken suburb west of Jacksonville. I searched for ammunition and equipment, not expecting much since part of the place was burned down and the rest looked pretty well looted. Figured I'd be in and out, ten minutes tops. Della and I had foraged together like that dozens of times, and I had no real reason to keep her out of it that morning.

Except for what had happened the night before.

A while after Mason died, things boiled over between me and Della. The night before Della and I reached Baker County and the burned out police station, we camped in a roadside stop abandoned while under construction. The place seemed free of the dead, maybe because no one living had been there when the dead plague started, but I knew if we stayed long enough, they'd come. We nested in a back storeroom with cinderblock walls, high small windows, and a solid, metal door, a place we could secure long enough to get some shut-eye. Sleep had been our plan, but sitting there in the silver moonlight, tension flowing out of us for the first time in days, we tumbled together as if drawn by gravity. Our lips grasped in long kisses that sent shivers through my body. We spread some blankets on the floor, stripped, placed our clothes on top of them to pad the icy tiles, and then we eased into the furnace of each other's heat.

Della felt firm and smooth. I relished her touch.

The pure silence that surrounded us was extraordinary, broken only by the rush of our breath, the whisper of our skin rubbing together, and our half-voiced moans of joy. We lasted quite awhile, each of us sparking the other through the ebb and flow of desire. We had a strange chemistry, the excitement of our first time together blended with the comfort of familiarity. Knowing death waited on every inch of ground we had to cover, in every second we had to live, bred intensity too; that plus our conviction we might be the last living man and woman in the world. I had never expected to experience anything like that. I don't think Della had either. If that had marked our last night alive, neither one of us would have been wholly dissatisfied.

The effect was powerful. It opened my eyes to the prospect of something more than a never-ending struggle to take another breath, travel another mile, and see another sunrise. I saw Della in a different light after that. The singular dread of the wormfeeders I'd lived with for so long now had company: my fear of letting down Della, like I had Evelyn and Mason.

So I made her wait in the car.

That's why the breath whooshed out of me and my blood froze when I came back empty-handed from the police station and saw she was gone.

FIVE

The sight of the empty passenger seat in Mason's car ran a spike of fear through me. I sprinted across the street and shouted Della's name. The car was clean; the doors were closed. Della's shotgun was gone. Hope flickered inside me. I clambered onto the front hood for a better view of the street and searched in every direction.

Nothing.

A dry breeze swept trash and debris along the vacant street. I waited for the noise of it rustling to die down then listened. Distant, shouting voices and the faint grumbling of a car engine came from the distance. *Sounds of living people.* My heart raced. A shotgun blast reverberated among the abandoned streets, booming as if its echoes alone might bring the buildings crumbling down around me.

I leapt from the car and bolted toward the nearest intersection in the direction of the gunshot. Around the corner and halfway down the next block Della stood on the steps of a cathedral, shotgun raised to her shoulder, a patch of silver smoke spreading from its barrels. The shadow of the steeple hid her target, but as I ran closer I saw two bodies: a man, dead but not yet reanimated, sprawled atop one of the walking dead, a woman, on the cathedral's granite steps. The man embraced the dead woman in a lifeless grip. Blood gushed from his neck, making islands of the scattered bits of his head on the stairs. The dead man's pants bunched down around his ankles, and the pale flesh of his rear stuck up in the air. He had managed to strap a gag around the mouth of the dead woman and tie her arms behind her back so he could get down to business.

"Sick bastard," I said.

Della snapped alert at the sound of my voice and waved her gun my way before she recognized me and lowered it.

"You all right?" I asked.

"I heard him howling," she said, trembling, her voice rising. "Kind of cheering, whooping it up. It's been so long since we saw anyone else living I wanted to check it out. I wanted to see another living person again. *This* is what I find! Damn it, months go by, we don't see another living soul, and then this is the shit I have to come out here and see!"

She screamed, her voice full of anger and horror.

I wrapped my arm around her shoulder and pressed her face to my neck. We held each other a moment and then I started walking, steering us away before the dead man came back.

"You did the right thing," I told her. "No telling what he might've done. Man like that can't be right in the head. Know what I mean? He's better off dead. You did him a favor."

Halfway down the block, I looked back and saw the dead man jolt upright, the skin of his face hanging inside-out over his chest like a soiled bib. His wormfeeder partner got up, too, hands behind her back. They played out a pitiful, clumsy bump and grind, working clear of each other and then shuffled after us, their desires of the flesh finally aligned.

"Time to go," I said, picking up the pace. "The police station was a bust, but we're not alone either. I heard voices and a car while I was looking for you."

We hustled back to the Camry to leave town, eager to avoid any other living people nearby, afraid the ones I heard might prove as sick as the man on the church steps. That's when something sharp and fast gouged a chunk of pavement out of the road three feet ahead of us and a gunshot cracked the air. Della and I crouched and dashed for the car as another shot buzzed between us and chipped the curb outside the police station. A third grazed Della across the shoulder, tearing her shirt and streaking a line of blood along her skin.

I spun and fired five shots in the direction of the sniper, buying us time to reach the car. Faint static crackled on a distant walkie-talkie. A man laughed through the heavy stillness and a second voice joined in, maybe two more after that. The shotgun blast had drawn whoever I had heard to come looking for us.

Della and I scrambled into the car and blasted off along the road. Our planned route called for us to double back toward the highway, a route now closed by the sniper, so we sped toward the other side of town, relieved when we left the buildings behind us and hopeful when we turned down that broken, desolate road, thinking it would lead us away from the madness. The road stretched ahead like a ribbon of concrete snakeskin; its barrenness should've been more than ample warning to steer clear, but I was too intent on getting out of town to notice.

About two miles along the way, we reached the blockade: a jumble of wrecked cars shoved into the road and crushed together under a telephone pole. From a hundred yards away I saw the shadows of men with guns moving on the other side of it. I hit the brakes, cut the wheel, and spun the car around, driving hard. We made it a quarter mile back the way we came before two pick-up trucks rolled into view, side-by-side, blocking the road, each one bearing an armed man mounted behind the cab, at least one of whom had sniped on us in the city, I guessed.

Right then I felt the presence of a nasty old friend of mine slinking back to my side, an unwelcome harbinger with dank, familiar breath that burned against the back of my neck; the hot, carrion air of the one I'd thought I'd left behind with memories of Evelyn and the madness of men who killed to rule over an empire of rot and dust.

My damn jackal returned, and I could smell his anticipation for whatever trouble now lay ahead of me.

SIX

I'm not a social person. People are too easy to manipulate, too ready to be misled, taken advantage of, and ridden herd, complacent so long as their basic needs are met, and willing to pay much more than required for the privilege. So the arrival of organized and armed men who'd tracked us out of town, discouraged me more than a little. Della and I held our guns out of sight on our laps and wondered if it might be better to hold tight and see what developed or burst out shooting and end this thing fast and clean. Going out in a blaze of glory would not have been a tragedy.

For a little while, no one made a move. Roadside pines swayed in the fast wind and dead maple leaves tumbled across the pavement. Horsehair clouds drifted above us. The faint aroma of the woods filled my nose, and time felt frozen, even as cold sweat dripped down my back.

A barrel-chested man jumped down from the closest truck, paused to adjust his belt, and then strolled halfway to our car. He knelt and set his rifle down on the double-yellow line, showed us a handgun he pulled from the back of his belt, and then placed it beside the first weapon.

He resumed walking.

I rolled down my window.

"That'll do," I called. "We can hear each other fine."

He stopped and smiled in the shade of his Marlins cap, his eyes hidden behind mirrored shades. "Well, listen to you giving orders," he said. "In case you hadn't noticed, friend, armed or not, my men and I got the upper hand here."

"Oh, is that how you see it?" I asked.

His smile faltered.

"Listen, we don't want any trouble with you and we don't intend to hurt you. Fact is we're kind of happy to see some other living folks. Been too long staring at the same faces down at our camp. We thought everyone else in these parts was dead and gone, that we were the only ones who survived."

"Oh, yeah? So, what, you and your snipers aimed to keep it that way?"

"No, no. It's not like that at all. We're real sorry about that. The shooting was uncalled for. A mistake. See, that was one of ours, a fellow named Cutter, your girlfriend shotgunned back by St. Pete's," he said.

"You saw what he was doing with that wormfeeder?"

The man nodded. His jaw tightened into a grimace.

"I did. That's why you two aren't dead. Probably would've done the same myself if I'd found him first. I suspected Cutter wasn't all right in the head, but he was cagey. We're better off without him poisoning the rest of us. If he's capable of that, who knows what he might do to one of our women or children."

I held my tongue.

"It's a harder world now than it's ever been," the man said. "Sometimes you have to kill the corruption before it spreads. I apologize for my snipers firing on you. Couple of the guys got a little overexcited before word went round who it was the lady shot and why. They had a good laugh afterward, though. Boys had a pool on how long that maggot would last." The man paused. A shadow of a grin bent his lips. "Big Mike won."

"Ain't that a joy for Big Mike," I said. "What the hell do you want with us?"

"Seeing as how we got off on the wrong foot here, let me introduce myself," he said. "Name's Tom Weichert, and despite what this looks like, I'm pleased to meet you."

"All right, then, Mr. Weichert. Let's chalk this up to a misunderstanding. Apology accepted. Been nice chatting with you, but now if you'll move your trucks, I think we'll head back the way we came and be on our way," I said.

"I wouldn't recommend that."

"Why's that?"

"You're heading south, planning to take the interstate, right?"

"What difference does it make to you?"

"None, really. But, see, I know you didn't come from the south, so I figure that's the way you're traveling. And about fifty miles along that way here there's a cluster of the dead. Got to be a hundred thousand or more crammed together around a little town down there called Baxton. They're all gathered there like it's some kind of party. Been hanging around six weeks or so, standing around decaying, as best we can tell. Waiting for fresh meat to show up, I guess. That's what you're heading into if you keep going."

I saw in Della's eyes that she believed Weichert's story. So did I. We had no reason to trust the man, other than the honest resonance in his voice and his unwavering eyes; the prospect of what he described chilled me. I'd never seen that many dead in one place. They tended to spread out and go wandering unless live humans attracted them to one place or another.

"Tell you what, here's my offer," Weichert said. "We got a place a little ways down this road, hidden, fortified, about a hundred and sixty of us living there. We keep the area clean by hunting scarecrows every day. We call the dead ones *scarecrows*. You want to spend some time with us, you're welcome. You prefer to take your chances on the road, that's your call and it's been nice meeting you. I wish you good luck."

Weichert gestured to the men behind him. Engines coughed to life and each truck pulled onto the shoulder, leaving the route clear.

I didn't hesitate in slamming my foot down on the gas, rocketing by so fast that Della squealed. Weichert flinched, grabbed onto his hat, and leapt backward. We shot between the trucks and blazed up the road, and no one fired a shot or so much as made a move to follow us. In the rearview I glimpsed the shock on Weichert's face and his men's puzzled expressions. Would've been easy enough for them to squeeze off a few pot-shots at us, try to cripple our car, but none of them even lifted a gun. No one tried to chase us. They simply stood there and watched.

I eased up on the accelerator and rolled to a stop.

"What's wrong?" asked Della.

"Think a minute," I said. "If what he says is true maybe we ought to hole up here a while and figure a better way to get south."

"Cornell, we don't need them," she said.

"No, we don't, I suppose, but we could use them to catch our breath, see if anyone knows what the hell is going on out there," I said. "If we have to wade through an army of wormfeeders to make it home, I'd like to have as much information as possible ahead of time."

Della considered it, her expression hardened by apprehension.

"I'm not sure I want anything to do with whatever it is they've got going on," she said.

"Thing is we need some real rest. We lost Mason because of a stupid mistake. I almost lost you this morning because of another one, leaving you alone like that, and then we drove down this dead-end road and got ourselves trapped. We aren't thinking clearly anymore," I said. "I'm no more excited than you are to meet the fucking neighbors, but we've got to stop moving for awhile and sleep more than a few hours here and there. We need to get our heads together and recuperate a little. Otherwise we got no chance at all getting through that many wormfeeders down the road."

"All right," Della said, but I could tell she didn't like it. "But we don't tell them where we're going, where we've been, or who we are. This is nothing long term for us. We're only visiting."

"Agreed," I said.

I turned the car around and drove back, noting the confused faces of the men as we rolled between the pick-up trucks and stopped beside Weichert. I cut the motor and stepped out.

"What the hell was that about?" he asked.

"Making sure your offer was sincere." I extended my hand and Weichert shook it. "We'd like to take you up on it. Name's Cornell and this is my wife, Della."

I don't know why I called Della my wife. Instinct took over and the words came out, but when I saw the subtle shift in Weichert's expression and felt his grip tighten around my fingers, I knew I'd done the right thing on that count. Up close and exposed something didn't feel right to me now. Della's warning jangled in my head. *We've been doing fine without these losers,* I told myself, but it wasn't true. We were on the edge. We needed a respite, and we couldn't be choosy about how we got it. Still, that didn't soften the hard rocky feeling in my gut telling me I'd just made my third dumb mistake that day and that this might be the big one. The jackal's laughing bark came rolling through my head, and I sensed his presence at my side, his muzzle so near my hand, I could almost feel the steam in his breath.

SEVEN

Weichert's pick-up led us down the road, me and Della following, the other truck bringing up the rear. The land around us bristled with overgrown honeysuckle twisting amidst sugar maple and blackhaw trees and tall pines, all of it shielded by waist-high grass growing along the shoulder. Here and there bits of glass and metal sparkled in the sunlight, the remnants of debris where wrecked cars had been hauled away to clear the road.

Out this way offered only wilderness. No stores, houses, gas stations, or farms, nothing but sun-cracked concrete and wild vegetation, probably infested with mosquitoes by the billions. I wondered what kind of encampment awaited us down the road and imagined a pathetic collection of faded tents and beat-up RVs. The farther we drove from town, the quieter Della got. I knew how she felt. We were weak prey if Weichert's men decided to jump us, but I didn't think that would happen. They could have done it right where they first stopped us, and Weichert seemed too straitlaced for that kind of shit.

Man liked his rules and kept his word. Saw that much in his eyes. No doubt that's how he got to be head of the pack with this simmering bunch that included a freak like Cutter. Weichert's men were all clean-shaven, wearing fresh clothes without stains or tears, good shoes, and carrying well-maintained weapons. They put on a nice, civilized show, but I smelled secrets scratching beneath its surface, and I wondered what Tom Weichert kept hushed up, waiting for a chance to air out or be buried for good.

The pavement ended at a three-foot drop down to soft ground, but Weichert's pick-up cut right and moved along a gravel trail hidden by brush. I followed. The car lurched and the tires spun when we hit a sharp incline, but then the treads caught and trundled us upward into a hollow of high pines and mottled shade. Six armed men, three along either side of the path, watched us. Della shrunk down in her seat.

"You still think we did the right thing?" she asked.

I didn't know, so I kept quiet.

Around a crook in the road stood a twelve-foot black bear carved from a pine trunk but looking fierce and alive in the dusty shaft of sunlight that angled down onto it. Twice the size any black bear ought to be and sporting a mean snarl, it startled me. A sign mounted at its feet read: Cady's Indian Museum and Nature Outpost.

We crested a hill and a cluster of six buildings came into sight. A sprawling brick mansion stood flanked by a cottage, a long garage, two large cinderblock and cement longhouses at the rear, and a brick station at the edge of a weed-pocked parking lot. Fifteen cars cooked in the sun, lined up in the spaces, all of them clean and looking ready to roll. People roamed the grounds out in the open as if the dead couldn't walk up and take a bite out of them any time. That disturbed me for its arrogance and foolishness—or maybe my subconscious only wanted to piss on the first rays of hope I'd felt in a long time.

I pulled in beside Weichert's truck. Della and I got out. The noontime breeze chilled my back where sweat had matted my T-shirt to my skin.

"Welcome to Camp Cady," Weichert said as he left the truck. "Not much but it's home." He laughed and slapped me on the back, flashing a smile better suited to an insurance salesman or a cocaine dealer.

"You folks are awful comfortable moving around in the open," I said.

Grinning, Weichert shook his head.

"Naw, we're safe here," he said. "We send hunting parties out daily to pick off any scarecrow comes within a few miles of the place. Long as they don't make it down here to the camp, they don't know we're here, and that keeps their numbers down and manageable. They're kind of like ants. Kill the scouts, the others go looking for food elsewhere. Being off the beaten path works in our favor in more ways than one. Couple months ago, an army troop came through town. They burned and foraged and mowed down scarecrows like twelve year olds at a shooting gallery. Fine enough, except then they came across a dozen or so living folks hiding out in the basement of an apartment building. They cleared them out. Killed half the men, took all the women, set the children loose, and kept on their way like a pack of coyotes following the scent of carrion. We watched from a distance. They never knew we were here. We took in a couple of the survivors afterward, those that wanted to go with us."

"The army's still online?" I asked.

Weichert shrugged. "Doubt it. These fellows looked rogue, maybe not even real army. Had the patches and insignia ripped off their uniforms. If they weren't on their own then I guess they have orders to survive and damn the civilians. Either way, it's all the same to us: no help there."

"What about Cady? He don't mind you setting up camp here?"

"If he does, he's not going to say much about it. Cady died about a month before the dead rose up. He was my friend, which is how I knew about his place. He was fixing to turn this into a tourist attraction. Developers planned for a shopping mall and hotel complex about two miles back up the road. Cady's family owned this land going back more than a hundred-and-fifty years. He figured the time had come to cash in. Built those longhouses and started up his collection of genuine Indian artifacts and museum-quality taxidermy displays. Got a hundred acres of nature trails out there, too. I'll give you and your wife the dollar tour later. Right now, though, let's get you checked in."

We crossed the parking lot with Weichert. Della stuck close and held my hand. Weichert ushered us into the squat building on the edge of the blacktop. Inside, three men sat behind desks piled with stacks of papers. They looked up in unison as Weichert introduced us.

"Figure on them being with us more than a few days," he said, and then he glanced at me over his shoulder, and asked, "Right?"

"Don't know," I said. "We're not looking to impose."

"No imposition," he said. "This isn't a free ride. We'll get files started for each of you, get you in the registry, and then interview you about what kind of skills you have. Depending on what we need done, these men will assign you work detail. Once that's set, they'll fix you up with quarters and you can start working tomorrow. Earn your keep fair and square and take your turns in the hunting rotation. That's how we do things around here."

"What kind of work?" Della asked.

Weichert winked at her. "Well, that's up to you, isn't it? What kind of skills you got, ma'am?"

Della glanced at me, waited for my slight nod.

"I'm a nurse," she said.

Weichert laughed. "That sure is welcome news. You'll be working over in the infirmary. See how easy it is? This is no tent city. The world we knew may be gone, but we're not savages. We've got to keep the building blocks of society alive, or else how will we rebuild? We have to preserve something to go back to when all this ends."

"What makes you think it ever will?" I asked.

"The dead got to rot away to nothing sooner or later."

"We've seen plenty look like they stopped decaying and started toughening up. If you're planning to wait this out, you may be rebuilding society from behind a walker."

"Heard rumors about that, reports from the hunting parties," Weichert said. "Well, we'll see, won't we? We're working on it. Meantime, you get yourselves all official and then get acquainted with some of the folks. You're permitted one weapon apiece in case any of the dead find their way here. Whatever else you're carrying goes in the armory."

"Fuck that," I said. "You're not taking our guns or anything else we own."

All affability fled Weichert's expression as it soured and tightened, and his face flushed sunburn red.

"Excuse me, Mr. Cornell, but I doubt you actually *own* any single item you're carrying. If you got receipts to prove it then fine, keep it. I understand people need to do what they can to survive, but that doesn't mean stealing and looting is condoned. It's only a necessary evil. We got a civilized community here and if you're with us then you're going to follow our laws. Someday the world will get back on track one way or another, and we're all going to have reckon for what we've done and taken. You got that?"

Two of Weichert's men dropped hands beneath their desks. I didn't have to strain to figure they were wrapped around guns.

I nodded, slow and deliberate, feigning resignation.

"Your camp, your laws," I said.

"Fine. Mind you something else. Got a good number of kids running around here, so we don't allow swearing in public. Do it again and you'll spend some time in the 'swear jar,' a small, dark place you won't like very much," he said. "Now that's out of the way, I'm happy to have helped you out today. I want us to be friends, but for now, maybe you'd better to think of me like most of the others do. I'm not some high-minded volunteer. I'm a duly authorized officer of the law for the great state of Florida, and until we get to know each other better, you can call me sheriff."

Weichert flipped back his jacket and revealed a bronze badge pinned to his shirt. Fuck my stupidity and fear and lack of confidence in finding a way for Della and I to weather whatever hell awaited us further down the road. I'd had enough of lawmen to last me until my hair turned white and my balls shriveled up back inside my body. It took a lot of willpower to stand my ground when I wanted to bust Weichert's nose then grab Della by the hand and run, but I knew we'd never make it down that winding gravel road, never reach the highway or the barricade before somebody squeezed off a lucky round to take us down. Della and I exchanged a quick glance, realizing in the same moment that we'd have to bide our time. And right then we started hating every fucking second of it.

EIGHT

They put us up on the third floor of the mansion, in a tiny clean room furnished with a nice bed. In the morning, sunlight streamed in through the windows. Married couples stayed together, which made me grateful for my improvised lie. Otherwise single women got the second floor and one of the longhouses, where Cady's museum displays had been cleared out and cubicles and cots had been set up; men took the other longhouse or roughed it in tents or under open sky. Weichert asked about our absent wedding rings, and I told him a group that jumped us back in Georgia had stolen them. That seemed to satisfy his curiosity.

Della's work in the infirmary made her feel good, and she telegraphed it in her face, in her walk, in how she smiled once in a while after going so long without smiling at all. The routine helped. So did getting a good night's sleep and having a safe place to be alone together. Mostly, though, I think that helping the injured nurtured Della's spirit; it gave her a way to fight back against the death and horror around us and reminded her that good things could still be done in the world and she could be part of them.

Weichert kept his word. He dumped most everything we had into "community ownership" for use as needed for the good of everyone at Camp Cady. They took our guns, some of our camping equipment and other supplies, but left us our clothes and personal belongings. I managed at least to hide the spare set of keys for the car. After that first day Weichert left us alone. We became two more faces among the crowd, two more names on a roster he needed to feed, shelter, and protect, of no special concern to him so long as we played by his rules. Few folks we met liked Weichert, but no one argued with his results keeping

Camp Cady organized and secure. The ones rankled by the rules vented their frustration on the daily scarecrow-hunting expeditions. I appreciated Weichert's cunning in giving folks a way to work out their anger by putting it to good use. Have to admit the man had a knack for leading the sheep and what he did wasn't all bad, either.

Della and I actually enjoyed ourselves there. We ate good meals together like normal people and hiked along the trails around camp in our off time. At night, cozy in our little room with the door locked and the windows open to the breeze, Della and I made love, moving like we had that first time, rediscovering the energy and passion that had drawn us together. Our bodies fit like they'd been tailor-made for each other, designed by fate. I cherished the scent of Della's hair, the texture of her skin, the taste of her on my lips, and the secret desires she whispered in my ears. Even when we lay side-by-side, spent, with the dawn creaking through the trees, we pressed our bodies together like parting would be a form of amputation.

Those first few days felt wonderful, but at the same time it chafed to remember what living—really living instead of concentrating on not dying—was all about, because I knew one day this too would end. Didn't matter how good or safe life was if it was living on someone else's terms, spending each day on a leash, no matter how slack or invisible. And that I wouldn't do anymore. With the world going to hell and death hiding in every shadow, that kind of life offered us little to be gained and everything to lose.

Della felt likewise. Most mornings she woke up before me, and I stayed in bed to watch her dress, savoring the way her taut body moved through the hazy sunlight in a muscular perfection of lines, curves, and shadows. Her skin gleamed, and when she breathed her chest rose and fell in measured time that hinted at her growing confidence. She became more meticulous in her habits, more reserved in her choice of clothing as she slipped back into a professional state of mind. The change worried me a little. I wondered if maybe she liked things at Camp Cady too much, but she always put my mind at ease without even trying with how she said things like "when we leave here" or "when we get down to your place in Lohatchie." She said things like that often and I took them to heart.

At the infirmary they mostly dealt with injuries—cuts, scrapes, sprains, and the like. Nothing too serious. Almost no one came in ill, which Della chalked off to the good weather, hard work, and the absence of pollutants in the air. The other infirmary workers told her they hadn't seen a patient with a cough, cold, or infection in months.

"I do feel bad for this one boy, though," Della told me one morning.

She sat brushing her hair in front of the mirror, dressed in only a pair of faded blue panties with her back half-turned to me while I reclined propped up on pillows.

"He's been in a bed since he got here about two months ago," she said. "Only twelve years old and he's on his own. Lost his family and everyone he had to wormfeeders. He got away but he broke his leg jumping out of a moving truck. Lucky someone found him out on the road and brought him here, but it was a bad break. He ought to be able to start walking again any day now, though. His name's Christopher. You can see in his eyes what he's been through. The way he stares off into space sometimes makes me think maybe it's even worse than the things you and I've seen, like it's aged him and there's an old man living inside him now."

I thought about the eyes growing from the brain of the wormfeeder that had killed Mason and the man Della shot on the cathedral steps, and I wondered what worse things the boy could've seen.

"Good thing, then, he's got you to care for him," I said. "You wait and see, get him up on his feet again and he'll be running around like a normal, healthy boy in no time, playing football, dreaming about girls. I promise."

"You should come visit him," Della said. "Not a lot of men come by the infirmary unless they're hurt, and I think he's getting tired of being mothered."

"Stuck in bed with a bunch of good-looking sympathetic women to wait on him hand and foot? The boy doesn't know how good he's got it," I said. "Give him another two years, he'll change his tune."

"Still, wouldn't hurt if you stopped by."

"I'll make a point of it," I said. "But mainly cause it'll give me an excuse to come by and harass your sexy ass. Drop by this afternoon, all right?"

Della smiled. She put her brush down then crawled back into bed and kissed my neck. Another minute and she was under the covers with me, slipping out of her panties, and we picked up where we'd left off only a few hours ago.

That's how it went most days, the two of us indulging in the luxury of not having to look over our shoulders every minute or put all our energy into keeping alive. Got so goddamn comfortable sometimes I started worrying I might be the one who'd want to stay at Camp Cady.

Lucky for me, though, I had Weichert and his cronies to make sure I never forgot what was going on in the world or where was the safest place for me and Della to plant our roots. They assigned me to work the greenhouse with a man named Birch, an ex-military scientist no one liked. I guess I brought it on myself to some extent. I didn't want Weichert to know what I'd really done in the past, so I'd told his people that I'd worked as a janitor. Thus, as a new guy with no special skills, I pulled duty as Birch's assistant. They joked when they told me where to go that they expected me to last no more than a day or two.

Birch's lab stood in a meadow a short hike through the woods, fixed up in an old greenhouse of glass and steel hidden from the compound's main grounds by overgrown orange groves. Most of the botanical supplies had been dismantled and set aside, replaced with Birch's equipment. My first day there I saw why everyone else avoided him. When he saw me coming, he stepped out from the greenhouse and greeted me by flipping me the bird.

"Hey, asshole, did Weichert send you down here to keep tabs on me?" he said. "Where does that hollow-headed mouth-breather think I'm going to run off to?"

"I'm supposed to assist you," I said.

"Piss off. I don't need assistance."

"Not that simple. I got a job to do, and I guess I ought to do it or risk the wrath of Sheriff Shithead." I pushed past Birch into the greenhouse. "Where do I start?"

Birch and I sized each other up. The dusty Special Forces insignia tattooed on his forearm gave me ample warning to not pick a stupid fight. At least we seemed to share an opinion of Weichert. I hoped that gave us enough common ground to get along. If Birch's grating personality had been the only thing driving people away, I could've toughed it out easily at the greenhouse, but that didn't tell the whole story. Birch also had the Wall, and that got under my skin. Birch gave me no warning about it. He let me go to work cleaning up, and I put in a good half-day's effort sweeping and getting piles of supplies organized before I reached that part of the greenhouse.

The Wall.

Where the body parts were hung.

Mixed in with ivy growing in the shadows in the back corner. Legs and arms. Hands. A pair of lungs. Several hearts. A head with no eyes, ears, or nose. Six loose eyeballs, wide and staring. And a selection of organs rotted beyond identification—all pinned up like a butterfly collection. You hardly noticed them when they kept still, but when the wind carried the scent of the living through cracked panes of greenhouse glass it set them all to stirring so the Wall came to life like a blanket of wriggling critters and insects.

Worst part was the eyes. Not the ones staked there for observation, but the ones that sprouted from the other specimens, the ones that stared out from lung tissue or rolled and blinked in withered cardiac muscle, the ones that watched me from the stump of a severed hand. They tracked me from beneath an oily film of putrescence. As Birch and I worked in the lab, the eyes marked our progress, silent, accusatory, their gaze palpable even to my turned back. My skin never stopped crawling in the greenhouse. That's the real reason no one wanted to work with Birch—that sensation of constant surveillance. No one wanted the dead watching them all day long.

Didn't seem to bother Birch, though.

Maybe he'd been pushed past the point of caring. Wherever he went, his eyes flickered like Christmas tree lights in the rain, and his scrub of gray hair clung to his skull like dried heather as if he hadn't thought to comb it for a week. He moved in fits and starts, standing stock still, lost in thought for minutes at a time before rushing to one part of his lab or another, fumbling with some inexplicable mechanism or some assortment of glass containers filled with sloshing fluids. He hardly ever glanced at the specimens or the eyes on the Wall except to take tissue samples. And he hardly ever spoke to me.

Birch gave me nothing but shit work and the silent treatment for a week, but I stuck it out because I enjoyed the solitude of the greenhouse, even if it meant working around Birch's dead specimens. Also, I figured if anyone at Camp Cady could tell me something I didn't already know about the dead it was Birch. Things between us brightened when I found his personal library on a back shelf. Not much, but it included Faulkner, Hemingway, O'Connor, even Jim Thompson, all in a small treasure trove of tattered paperbacks. I had never put much stock in school and all its bullshit, but reading kept my mind sharp. Half of what had put me three steps ahead of the cops and the feds during my days robbing banks I'd learned from books, and I'd even tried my hand at writing now and then. I asked Birch if I could borrow a couple novels. He nodded, and the next day, we started talking books. That stabilized things between us; it gave us a basis for communication.

One day I told Birch about the eyes I'd seen in the brain of the dead man who'd killed Mason as well as the eyes I'd seen in other wormfeeders.

"Happens all the time," he told me. "I've been studying it since the beginning. I keep hoping it'll lead me to some answers, but I only wind up with more questions. The hunting parties keep me supplied with plenty of test subjects, but I hang on to the bits and pieces that grow eyes the longest. Burn the rest when I'm done with them."

"Weichert says you're working on 'a cure for not dying when you die,'" I said.

Birch laughed. "There's no cure. Weichert is a man whose mind works in two modes: black and white. His world fits together like a crossword puzzle, and he thinks if he plugs in all the right letters, everything will make sense and order will be restored. In his mind, everything happens for a reason, and I don't mean that in a pussy 'oh, it was meant to be' kind of way.

With Weichert, there's a bump in the night, it's because someone knocked. You get what I'm saying?"

"Yeah, he's the original problem solver," I said. "No mysteries. Find the cause, you find the cure."

"Exactly. Catch is, there's no cause," Birch said. "At least nothing scientific like Weichert thinks. There ought to be, sure. He's right as far as that goes. And I can tell you with an unfortunate degree of certainty that I've come closer than anyone alive to finding it. So close, in fact, that I know it simply isn't there to be found. I can describe some of the mechanics involved. I can tell you some of how the dead are walking but not the why. It's like understanding that people need lungs to breathe air but not knowing what oxygen is or how it transfers to your blood or why we even have lungs to begin with."

"You did all that here?" I said.

"No." Birch grinned without humor. "I used to be VP for research at Vanguard Biotech, a company with a shitload of military contracts and the direct attention of the president. When the dead plague started, they sent a tank brigade to our facility to protect us so I could keep working. Got as far as identifying a mutated tetanus virus as the key mechanism involved with muscular function in the dead before the worm-feeders drove us out of there. Now, I'm doing my best with what I've got here, but the only way I can describe what's happening is that time stands still for the dead on a cellular level. Decay slows almost to the point of cessation. But as for what's keeping them moving, making them feed off the living, I'm stumped."

"So? Seals don't ask sharks why they want to eat them," I said. "By now the dead must outnumber the living, anyway. This world is more theirs than ours."

Birch stared at me for several seconds, seeming to slip into some mental tar pit, but then he climbed back out of it and nodded. "Yeah, it is." He went back to work and didn't speak another word the rest of the day.

On my two-week anniversary, Birch told me no one else had worked with him that long, then declared it time for a celebration. He slapped me on the back and steered me to the far side of the greenhouse and a cabinet from which he produced a bottle of Johnnie Walker Black and two glasses. We sat in wide-backed wicker chairs, surrounded by ferns, and Birch poured.

"Glad to have you around," he said

He threw back half his drink.

"I appreciate the work," I said, following suit.

"Tell me something," Birch said. "Weichert pick you up on the road near town?"

"Yeah." I told him the story of how Della and I came to Camp Cady.

"Most folks knew Cutter would need putting down sooner or later," he said. "But listen, some free advice. Don't get too comfortable here if you value your principles or your sanity. This isn't 'Cady's Indian Museum and Nature Outpost' anymore. It's 'Tom Town.' That's what I call it since Tom Weichert's started running it like a tin tyrant. You got anyplace else to go, do yourself a favor and go there. Clean sheets and hot food have their appeal, but things will boil over here sooner or later. Leaving before then will make your life a lot easier in the long run, especially if you can look out for yourself out there."

"A comfortable prison is still a prison," I said.

"There it is in a nutshell."

"Yeah, that's about my sense of things," I said. "Trouble is I don't know if the good sheriff is ready to let us go. My wife's a hell of a nurse. Word is she's been a godsend in the infirmary. Besides, we were heading south."

Birch frowned.

"The first problem I might be able to help you with, but if you're heading south, well, then maybe you don't have anywhere else to go. Forty, fifty miles south the dead are gathering. Something big brewing down at Deadtown, a place called Baxton. The damned scarecrows are shambling in by the thousands."

"I heard. What's it all about?"

"Damned if I know, but don't tell Weichert. He thinks I'm working it all out so I can hand him a big fat report three weeks from Tuesday."

We drank again, and I enjoyed the soft burn of good liquor. A light drizzle fell and pattered against the glass and the leaves overhead. It turned the air damp and chilly. Whiskey warmth filled me, and I didn't object when Birch refilled our glasses before he put the half-full bottle away. I stared through the glass ceiling where smoky, furrowed clouds swept over swaying treetops.

"Tell me for real," I said. "What's with the eyes?"

Birch cleared his throat. "What do you mean?"

I straightened up and studied his craggy face, its lines deepened by the afternoon gloom. He knew more than he wanted to tell. I'd suspected it for a few days, but seeing his face then, I knew it. He hid it well, but my survival and my livelihood used to depend on solid snap judgments of people. It helped to know whether or not an assistant manager was lying about not being able to open a bank vault before you pushed a gun in his face to persuade him to do so.

"I mean," I said, "what makes those eyes pop up like that?"

Birch's gaze drifted toward the trails of rainwater snaking down the outside walls.

"Magic," he said.

"Is that so?"

I walked over to the Wall. It bothered me the way Birch had everything strung up, mounted, and spread out over an eight-foot span. The limbs and bits of flesh resembled a man pulled apart alive, only I knew nothing living hung there, only mute and mindless scraps of what had once been life.

"Acid works," Birch said. "To destroy them, I mean. So does fire. Lye. Anything that causes irreparable cellular damage. Microwaves work. Dries them right up. Shooting them or cutting them slows them, makes it hard for them to function. Told Weichert what he needs are flamethrowers or some pesticide tanks filled with acid, but he's holding out for a panacea. Thinks he can get his hands on some crop dusters and spray a miracle cure far and wide. Man's got visions of reclaiming the entire Panhandle and running it like his own little kingdom."

The Wall repulsed me, yeah, but it drew me in too with its constellations of eyes, their glistening pupils growing and shrinking with the light, dead flesh straining to blink. I couldn't imagine how they could see without a brain to process the image, but I sure as hell felt seen.

Birch laughed. "You got some balls to get that close."

"Don't worry. I'm well acquainted with this sort of bullshit," I said. "Tell me about magic."

A thick chuckle rolled out of Birch's throat.

"I mean it," I said. "What? Like ghosts? Voodoo?"

Birch's face adopted the bone-weariness that until then had only been apparent in the cast of his shoulders and the tepid resignation in his voice.

"Nothing like that. I've got some theories. None that'll solve Weichert's problem. I've worked on the why long and hard and I've come to the conclusion that it's a matter beyond science," he said. "Unless you want to believe the basic laws of physics and biology can be broken or made to change on an individual basis."

"I don't follow," I said.

"It's like I told you. Time is standing still for the dead, so they're not rotting. You've heard of relativity? Imagine ten seconds go by. Ten seconds pass in the world while maybe one, or one-tenth, or one-one-hundredth, or one-one-thousandth of a second passes for these dead fuckers up walking around and making our lives miserable," Birch told me. "Can you explain that? I sure as hell can't. That doesn't even touch on why they're ambulatory or need to eat live flesh. I'm trained to look at the world in a rational way, to seek the underlying reason things are how they are, the mechanisms that drive reality. But as far as I can tell, what's happening with the dead is a cosmic whim or the result of some fundamental alteration in the nature of existence. *Magic.*"

I gestured to Birch's equipment on the greenhouse tables. "You can tell all that from this little kitchen chemistry set you got here?"

"You haven't seen downstairs," Birch said. "I've got all the equipment I need plus two generators Weichert endlessly bitches about keeping fueled to run it all. Took most of it from my old lab. Before the dead rose up I was working on the highest profile stuff, my friend. Things the mainstream would say were fifty, sixty years out, all top secret, all rather dire and revolutionary, and one or two patently illegal under international laws, but hey, I never let that stop me cashing my big, fat paycheck. Before all that, I did things in the Special Forces—*saw* things— before I went back to school and got into the lab. That all gave me a rather finely tuned set of instincts for sorting fact from horseshit. So, believe me when I tell you that if there's a biological reason for the dead to be walking, I'm the man who would've found it."

"So what's the sticking point? You said you had some theories."

Birch scowled and hunched forward.

"You really want to know? I think there's *no* scientific reason. The dead come back to life because, for lack of a better word, God—whatever he, she, or it may be—*willed it so*. The universe is dying on the vine. This is all part of its great, last gasp. You and I are nothing but pallbearers who've overstayed our welcome at the funeral, nothing but carrion crawlers and dung beetles surviving on the remains. Corpse fauna. If we're lucky the Almighty won't forsake us altogether when he finishes with all his killing and resurrecting. In fact, I think despite appearances he's not even close to done with us yet."

The scientist sipped from his glass and sank back into his chair. I set my drink on the table and rubbed my eyes.

"How do you know you're right? Take it on faith?"

"I don't have any faith," he said. "I've seen this—out there in the ranks of the dead, in here when I look into their eyes, and their flesh, and into their cells. I've seen it in my dreams. I've seen and heard things I don't think any man was ever intended to know. Maybe I'm fucking nuts. Maybe I'm plain wrong. But if I'm not, then about fifty miles south of here where the dead are gathering in their masses, they're getting ready to write the epitaph for an entire world and maybe countless others beyond. It's some fucked up shit, believe me, but you asked, and now you know why I'm leading Weichert along and keeping this to myself. I don't want to make poor Tom's head explode."

I smirked. "I'd like to see that."

"Me, too, now that I think about it."

Neither of us laughed, though.

No matter where I went, I wound up with the law to my left and God to my right, and true to form neither side was playing nice with the other. Once again I found myself caught between the slavering jaws of the same beast that I'd thought I'd left behind in prison. I pined for the road, to be alone with

Della, barreling down the ruins of highways no one cared about anymore, the sky and the earth our own to do with as we pleased, and no one to get in our way. Birch called earth dead; I thought maybe it could be the Garden of Eden. And right then I started planning how Della and I were going to make it back to paradise.

NINE

Weichert volunteered me for a hunting party. All the men took turns in rotation, but he bumped me to the head of the list after I lasted two weeks with Birch. My hitting it off with the scientist irked him, and he wanted to remind me who was in charge. Della hated the idea of me going into the woods with Weichert's men. She didn't trust them or Weichert, and she worried I might never come back, leaving her stranded at Camp Cady.

We'd been talking about leaving in another week, maybe two, and our plans had gotten more complicated. Della wanted to bring Christopher. The kid reminded her of her dead brother, and he talked to no one but her about his experiences. She wouldn't tell me what he said. I didn't press it.

I hung out with Christopher now and then. We shot the breeze about rock music, and the walking dead, and how he wanted to grow up and race cars, and though it seemed impossible he'd ever get the chance, I liked that he still had a dream. He was a skinny, picture-perfect kid with fine, unruly hair, the kind of boy I could picture swinging off a long rope into a cool lake on a July afternoon, the kind girls would be all over when he was old enough. A smart kid, too, and I liked him, but I didn't see the upside to him hitting the road with Della and me. Chances were good not all of us would live to see Lohatchie, and Christopher would probably do better staying put. I was enough of a realist to accept that; Della wasn't. Except where Weichert's intentions toward me were concerned, she clung to her optimism.

Despite her worries, though, I saw no way out of my going on the hunt.

I tried to ease Della's mind by pointing out that sending me off to the woods to be killed wasn't Weichert's style. He wanted to break me. The man was a prick but not a cold-blooded killer. Everyone at Cady's lived in Weichert's shadow, and he liked it that way. It showed in their guarded expressions and furtive conversations, in their efficiency and conformity calculated to keep them off Weichert's radar. I saw how unhappy most of them were, except Weichert's inner circle of "trusted deputies." That's what he called the men who kept the rest of us in line. Life at Camp Cady was so well ordered and polite, folks hardly hollered when they stubbed a toe, and Weichert had to know that with the strings pulled that tight, a revolt could erupt any time.

So I didn't expect him to pull something clumsy like staging a hunting accident to get rid of me. I hadn't challenged him openly, but he understood what kind of threat I might be to his rule now some of the others had started to look up to Della and me. Della had bandaged up a lot of injured folks, and my lasting so long with Birch amazed people. They thought I worked hard every day to find a cure. Weichert watched us, gauged our influence, our potential to challenge him, and he wanted to smack me down. I could eat that if it bought us time to make our escape.

The morning of the hunt, sun poured down from a pristine sky and baked my skin. Three days of rain had broken in the night, leaving the ground soft and the air damp with the perfume of pines and wet loam. The heat would dry it soon enough. Six of us trekked out, led by a deputy named Wrigley, driving a pick-up as far into the woods as the terrain permitted, and from there we continued on foot. Each of us carried a handgun, a rifle, ammunition, a machete, and a day's worth of food and water. One man led two mutts on long leashes, our early alert system: Canine noses would smell the wormfeeders long before we could and dogs got skittish around the dead.

Trudging single file through the mud we marched a couple of hours over grassy slopes and fields until we reached the bank of a marsh. An odor of rot wafted off the stagnant water, and the air buzzed with a haze of flies and gnats. We circled to the far side, swatting insects the whole way, and then picked up the trail, which ran narrower and rougher on the other side of the marsh. By then we'd traveled twelve or fifteen miles from the compound, moving in burdensome silence and sweating under the high sun.

Our concentration turned razor sharp for signs of movement in the brush, for the dogs to bark or whine, for the telltale stink of the dead. And when it came it hit like a gale coming off a sun-cooked landfill.

The hounds dug in and refused another step down the trail. Bared their teeth and growled so loud their keeper trotted them back the way we came before they gave away our position. The rest of us crept forward to where the path widened through a stand of pines and led toward cottony brightness and shadows filled with movement among the tree trunks.

"There's a meadow on the other side of those pines," Wrigley whispered. "We scatter, move up, weapons ready. Hunker down just this side of the trees. Fire on my order. Cripple them and then we go in close for the hack-and-burn work. Everyone got it?"

We crept through the dead stench that billowed around us thick as smoke from a tire fire. A chorus of moans cried out from lifeless throats, rising and falling in a way that reminded me of the losing team's fans at a football game. A buzzing current underpinned it, white noise like electrical lines humming on a rainy day. The men swapped anxious glances, everyone edgy but too uncertain to speak up. Good thing I wasn't.

I gripped Wrigley's shoulder and said, "Wait."

The deputy snapped around, surprised, jittery. He glared at me. I dropped my hand, gave him some distance.

"Cut the crap, Cornell. You got your orders."

"Use your head," I said. "Smell that? Hear that? A few strays wandering by don't put up that much stink and noise. Got to be a mob of them, dozens, maybe more. You want to walk right into that?"

"Can't be a mob. We never get that many scarecrows back here. No reason for them to come this way," he said.

A man named Farmer inched forward and spoke. "You're right, Deputy, but so is Cornell. Okay? We've all been on enough of these hunts to know something's different, here. Damn stink is making my eyes water. You ever see the dogs tense up that way before?"

Wrigley flashed me a "see what you started" kind of look, but then he wandered a few feet farther down the trail, dropped to his haunches, and listened. Languid wind shook the pine needles and a bird called from somewhere far away, a delicate musical sound against the groaning of the dead.

Wrigley returned with a hard expression, and said, "You best be right, Cornell, or Tom will hear about your insubordination."

The threat rang hollow, words to keep face even if he knew they were bullshit.

"I can live with that," I said.

"All right, then, here's how we do it," Wrigley said. "We creep up to the tree line, stick to the shadows, hang fire, and see what we're dealing with. Y'all can handle that? Y'all feel better this way? Bunch of tired, fucking pussies I got backing me up."

I smirked and said, "Language, Deputy. What would Sheriff Weichert think hearing you swear like that?"

Farmer and the others chuckled, and the tension eased, but Wrigley sneered at me before he led us down to the edge of the trail. We crouched on hands and knees, nestled into the high grass encroaching from the field, concealed behind a jumble of deadfall. Past the pines the dirt trail cut into a deep, concave meadow. Grass bleached dry and pale by sunlight practically glowed as it swayed in the breeze, flitting back and forth like the golden tongues of a million snakes. Through it shambled an unbroken line of corpses, their rag clothing flapping from their decomposing bodies, their flesh gray, black, and purple in the searing daylight, their wounds that would never heal rippling with maggots and flies. The noise of a billion carrion crawlers hummed among the moans of the dead. The fresher corpses still resembled men and women, but most had deteriorated beyond distinguishing features although the filthy ruins of a necktie or a bra strap or a nametag provided an occasional clue. Children stood out, but nobody wanted to look at them. The line shuffled along, a thread of guided chaos, eight or ten bodies wide, stamping the grass flat, killing it as they followed a well-worn route. They moved slow and steady, shuffling and lurching, their shriveled eyes and empty skull sockets fixed on an unknown point to the south. Wrigley took a pair of field glasses from his belt and gazed northward in the direction of the column's source.

"Shit and piss in a blender," he said.

He passed the glasses to Farmer, who stared through them for several seconds and then handed them to me. I raised them and looked. On and on walked the dead, coming from as far as the eye could see, a distance of maybe a couple miles with every indication that the line reached much farther than that, stretching toward a hidden source maybe fifty miles, maybe a thousand to the north. The corpses passed out of sight south of us. This forced march of the damned, this measured torrent of rot and decay, this scar upon the quiet earth—the sight of it drove home what Birch had said about the living being like carrion bugs infesting nature's new order. We were six living men against an irresistible wall of moving dead flesh, and I didn't need to see the others' faces to know how small each and every one of us felt in its presence.

Some of the wormfeeders slowed down as they passed our position. Those trailing them bumped into them. They danced clumsy circles for a few minutes, tangled up in one another, until one of them fell over and broke the clog. The others stomped along, crushing his twitching body into the soil, but more came and got hung up right there in front of us, distracted from their journey. It was clear our presence threw them off. They sensed us.

As silent as we'd come, we retreated up the trail, hoping we hadn't lingered long enough for them to follow. Past the marsh the path rose to a low hill and we dug in there for a couple of hours to make sure the dead wouldn't track us back to Camp Cady. None of them came up the trail, though, and when we felt sure none would, we hurried back to the pick-up, jogging every other mile to reach it before dusk.

The whole ride home Wrigley rambled on, without really saying anything, asking himself all sorts of pointless questions as he tried to find some explanation for what we'd seen. The rest of us kept quiet, sifting the murk of our own thoughts. No one wanted to voice it but the meaning loomed clear. Baxton, where the dead gathered, stood to the south. We hadn't stumbled upon a random migration but a pilgrimage with a known destination. That meant something no one had yet guessed—that meant the rotting scarecrows, the mindless dead, the stinking, fucking wormfeeders walked with a purpose.

TEN

Credit where credit is due: Weichert played the hand dealt him as well as anyone could once my hunting party returned with news of what we'd seen. He met with his deputies then ordered them to spread word to the others a few small groups at a time so as to put everyone on guard without sparking a panic. He organized eight armed groups, four men each, to camp at posts three miles outside the complex and stand guard in the direction of the dead march. A rotation of scouts placed deeper in the woods kept watch on the walking corpses. They did their best to protect us, no doubt, but they guarded the wrong place. Three days after my hunting party gave its report, my initial fears about Camp Cady being so open and exposed proved right on the money.

A wormfeeder wandered into camp, but it came from the direction of the highway not the deep woods and the dead march. Most likely it crossed the parking lot, strolled by the cars, and stumbled over the rough ground there before it trudged up to the front door of the mansion. It came in the early morning, and no one saw it. Posting so many men to the west left the eastern perimeter vulnerable. A woman, Nancy Morris, leaving the mansion must have walked head on into the thing, and judging by the state she turned up in later, the wormfeeder tore open her throat before it dragged her to the ground and started gnawing into her stomach. It fed for a while, leaving a pile of organ scraps we found and burned later, slurping down what it could until three children turned up the walk and disturbed it. They took one look, screamed, and fled. Smart kids. Too bad they didn't have a decent weapon among them to end things before they really got started. The wormfeeder chased after them, leaving its fresh kill to clamber onto her feet a couple minutes later and wander to the infirmary, dragging her guts through the dirt.

The children evaded the first corpse, and a little later it wandered by the old gazebo where Chester Lang was making repairs. The carpenter fought back with a hammer, caved in the wormfeeder's skull, smashed its brain, and then chopped the thing down to manageable bits with a hatchet, coming away with

a dozen or so nasty bite wounds and a gash along his abdomen—
but he lived.

Across the compound dead Nancy Morris got as far as the
open grass outside the women's longhouse, which housed
the infirmary. Della saw her first. While everyone else scrambled
to lock the place down, she stepped outside with her gun drawn
and put two rounds through dead Nancy's head. That took her
off her feet long enough for Della to pin her down with an ax then
go to work with a scalpel and a hacksaw, concluding poor Ms.
Morris' existence as a mobile flesh-eating corpse. Della took her
apart the way she'd done so many others back when she pulled
disposal duty in the prison infirmary. That should've ended it,
but all the activity over the intrusion meant no one noticed three
more wormfeeders coming from the east, proving my rule that
nowhere ever stands really free of the dead.

Rotted down to little more than bone and ligaments in places,
they crawled out of the woods and crossed the camp like giant
beetles clacking for prey. They found their way to the garage
where each one killed a man. Of course, their victims rose, driven
by a sudden hunger for flesh, and so six wormfeeders roved into
the heart of Camp Cady. A lot of people died before the sheriff
put the lid back on, and yeah, we can call that a loss and a big,
bad day for Tom Weichert and his almighty rule of law. It took
Weichert's men two hours to round up all the dead ones and
when the last had been put down and burned, the body count
numbered twenty-three residents, including four killed by stray
shots fired by Weichert's deputies. A riot almost broke out then
and there, but it had been so long since most folks at Camp
Cady had seen a wormfeeder that shock trumped outrage. That
wouldn't last long, though. The illusion of happy life at Cady's lay
shattered.

Down at the greenhouse, hard at work in the cellar, Birch
and I missed the ruckus. I only heard about it later from Della.
That night we decided we ought to leave in another day or two,
three at most.

"Camp Cady is not a safe haven anymore," she said. "What's
the point in hanging around? Besides, Christopher is ready to
travel now."

I wrapped my arms around her, reveling in the flush of having made love and not wanting to talk about such stuff but knowing Della was right.

I said, "It's a good idea. The dead march isn't that far from us. Only a matter of time before some of them wander this way and the secret about this place gets out. Only thing is Birch has been up to something new, and I'm curious to find out what. He hasn't been this intense about anything since I met him."

"Well, tell him to hurry it up. I've been swiping supplies from the infirmary, putting together a little stockpile," she said.

"Like old times."

Della laughed. "We'll need some food, too, and our camping gear and stuff, and weapons."

"The car," I said. "Got to figure a way to load up and sneak out of here without getting shot. Birch said he might be able to help us with that. I'll talk to him tomorrow."

"You think he ought to come with us?"

I shook my head. "Doubt he would. And, anyway, I like him, but I'm not sure his deck is full anymore."

"That woman who died today," said Della. "She sprouted eyes everywhere when I started cutting her up. Every time I took off one of her limbs an eye blinked back at me. It made me feel like cold beetles were crawling under my skin. Whatever's behind those hated me. I felt it, no doubt in my mind. Cold, stony hate. I sliced the eyes to stop them from looking at me, but more kept popping up, in all the wormfeeders. It's getting worse than it ever was."

I told her about the Wall and some of Birch's ideas. She listened, her quiet body warming me, her gentle breath brushing my neck, her heartbeat thudding against my chest.

"I don't care what they are or what they want. I only want to get away from them," she said. "Promise me, all right? That we'll go away from here, away from all this horror, and find our own, safe place? Okay?"

"I promise," I said.

I kissed her and slid my hand along her body, feeling her heat. She welcomed my touch.

The next morning I made Della wake up early and after a stop by the infirmary to pick up Christopher, I took her and the boy into the woods to the place where Weichert had dumped all of Cady's taxidermy displays when he'd had the longhouses cleared out for housing. Cady had been a real enthusiast and so the three of us stood amidst animals from six different continents, each one expertly preserved though now soiled and frayed from being left outdoors, torn and punctured from being used for target practice. Among them were two black bears; an array of big cats that included a leopard, a tiger, and some cougars; an alligator and a crocodile; three spider monkeys; two wolverines; a group of raccoons; a wolf, a dingo, and one other to which I felt a special attachment: a jackal.

It looked exactly like the one in my head.

With their fur matted down, paws spattered with mud, and dry leaves clinging to them, the animals looked all the more lifelike. I expected them to come to life like the dead, but they never did. Every so often, I glanced over my shoulder at the jackal and could've sworn I felt him looking back. Della didn't know about the jackal, and I didn't tell her. Sharing that kind of secret can change how people think of you, not often for the better. Besides, we had work to do. Birch had given me a set of hunting knives. I handed one each to Della and Christopher and showed them how to use it. Science wasn't all Birch and I had been up to down at the greenhouse.

"He doesn't like to talk about it, but Birch was in the Special Forces," I said. "He adapted his military, hand-to-hand combat training to fight the dead close up. He made a system of cutting them so their joints are left useless but you don't have to sever their limbs. We learned the hard way a legless body can still drag itself across the ground and bite you. A severed hand or arm can still claw you. Just like with Mason. Birch says you sever the spine to burden them with their own dead weight. Then you clip the shoulders and hips the right way, and you got a trunk straddled with limbs like a plastic doll whose rubber bands have snapped. Takes them right down. Since they're half dried out already, you can slice into them a lot deeper than you'd be able to cut a living person."

I showed them what Birch had taught me: the proper way to hold the knife, how to thrust, to slice, where to place the blade, how to keep moving so they couldn't grab you. Then we practiced the motions.

"Don't cut too deep. You might get your blade stuck or cut the limb all the way off," I said.

"I'm not that strong," said Della.

"Strength's not the only factor. A lot of the dead are rotten inside," I said. "Five blows is a lot, I know, but the worm-feeders are slow. It works if you keep your head and stick to the pattern."

"What if there are too many?" Christopher asked.

"Run," I said. "Nothing else you can do."

"Why don't we just shoot the fuckers?"

Della smacked the boy in the back of the head. "What'd I tell you about watching your mouth?"

"Give me a break," Christopher said. "We're out here learning how to slice up living corpses in five easy steps, and you get on my case about swear words?"

I grinned and said, "Little fucker's got a point."

Della scowled at me for a moment, then turned away to hide the smile creeping into her face. "You boys must be closer in age than I thought."

"You know how to use a gun?" I asked Christopher.

"My brother taught me. I'm a good shot."

"All your family could handle one?"

"Sure. We learned after the dead started walking."

"How many wormfeeders were there the last time you saw all your family alive?" "Cornell, don't," Della said.

"It's all right," I said. "I need to make a point about thinking a gun in your hands is a magic wand that's going to solve all your problems. They got in close, right? Overran you. You couldn't get in a good crippling shot, and one bullet, even at point blank range, doesn't do much to them does it? Maybe you ran out of ammo, no time or room to reload, and then all you had was a club, something blunt they could grab, two or three of them latching on to pull it away from you. Did it happen something like that?"

The exuberance left Christopher's face. His stony glare made it clear I'd struck a nerve. His mussed, sandy hair twitched in the breeze, and he looked more like a child in that moment than any other time I laid eyes on him. He looked little and lost. His eyes welled up a bit, but he squelched his tears.

"Guess a knife is a handy thing," Christopher said, his voice a hair above a whisper.

"Save your life, maybe," I said.

Christopher stepped toward me. "Show me that last move again, okay?"

After that we practiced a while longer. Della never uttered another word about what I'd said to Christopher. The two of them caught on quick. Our blades flashed through the shadows and sunlight time and again until they knew the pattern as well as I did. When we finished, I turned and hurled my knife into the jackal, landing it dead in the side of the thing's neck. A puff of dust spewed out but the jackal didn't come to life or snarl as I saw it in my mind. Its glass eyes bored through me, stale, indifferent, staring straight into forever as if nothing in the world could ever kill their owner. I'd never seen a real, living jackal, but I couldn't imagine there would be any more life in its eyes than I saw in this one's.

ELEVEN

Weichert held it together for two days before he showed up at the greenhouse, bright and early, stepping through the door while Birch and I spiked our coffee with a touch of Johnnie Walker. The mood at Camp Cady remained bleak. The sheriff waited inside the door for a minute, watching us through the lattice of morning shadows. Then he glanced once at the Wall and shivered before averting his gaze to a row of African violets Birch cultivated. He eyeballed Birch's gadgets and experiments in progress spread out all over the long plant tables as he approached us.

"Time for a talk, fellows," he said.

Weichert's tone bore a touch less antipathy and a few degrees less arrogance than usual, undoubtedly due to the humbling security breakdown, maybe even an aftereffect of Wrigley reporting how I'd helped the hunting party stay alive. I think Birch sensed it too, because he refrained from the usual verbal lashing he saved up special for Weichert. Or maybe he mellowed only because he hadn't had his coffee yet. Either way, I suppose it's true: troubling times bring folks closer together, at least where their instincts for self-preservation converge.

"All right," Birch said. "Want some coffee?"

He filled another mug from the pot and then tipped the whiskey bottle over its rim, pausing a moment to see if Weichert would object, then letting the honey-colored liquor splash into the dark brown brew. That emptied the bottle.

He handed the mug to the sheriff, and said, "Let's talk in the lab."

Birch had spent more and more time in the greenhouse cellar over the past week, and it gave him a home field advantage. He hadn't lied about his equipment. I couldn't name half his machines and gadgets, but Birch worked them like a virtuoso, setting them up, priming them, letting them run, and making sense of the results. He recorded his data on three laptop computers and a dozen notebooks scattered around, each one dedicated to a different research path. I'd tried reading them but Birch's tech jargon and calculations only got jumbled up in my head. As best I understood, Birch resumed looking for a viral or bacteriological factor, re-treading work he'd done months ago in hopes of spotting some overlooked detail or finding new inspiration. He fixated on the idea of bacteria already present in human cells but only activated when its host expired, perhaps even by some other bacteria that thrived in decaying human tissue. Not that he had changed his views on what really fueled the resurrection, but he seemed driven by sheer intellectual curiosity. Birch the man might not have needed answers, but Birch the scientist couldn't stop asking questions. Despite his beliefs, he tortured himself working every angle that might unlock the secret of the reanimated dead, and I believed him when he said if there was a reason to be found under a microscope or in a test tube that he would've found it by then. A man like that—who's exhausted all rational options, who's sweated blood working to prove himself wrong—well, when he tells you there's only one answer to be had, no matter how much you hate the idea of what he's saying, you know odds are he's right. A man like Weichert, on the other hand, a man hell-bent on reconstructing an impossible way of life—he won't accept anything that doesn't fit his crystal clear, box-framed picture of the world no matter how bold the evidence. Put the two together and there's nothing to do but sit back and wait for the shouting to die down. At least things started off calm.

"We lost good people the other day. I let everyone down. Did my best, but I still let them down. I'm man enough to admit my best didn't cut it," Weichert said. "Now everyone's scared, and I need some answers, fast, to keep things from falling apart."

Weichert's humility surprised me. Birch, too, I think, because he hesitated before he answered, and when he did, he spoke with genuine regret.

"I'm sorry, Tom. I'm really sorry that I can't help you more, that I've got no good answers for you. But I don't have enough information to know anything for sure and you don't like my theories," Birch said.

Honest, yeah, but not what Weichert wanted to hear.

Weichert had put himself at Birch's mercy. Maybe he thought Birch was holding out on him, keeping back information out of spite, and if he only admitted how much he needed Birch's help then the scientist would grant it. For Weichert, humility and desperation made for uncomfortable companions. His face reddened, he snapped at Birch, and then the conversation tensed up fast. Their verbal artillery escalated, and in minutes, their shouting filled the room. Each man jabbed at the other's insecurities and fears; neither gave an inch. Though they had known each other less than six months, they argued like old men who've been taking each other to task decade after decade until they don't know any other way to communicate but to fight. They wanted to help each other, sort of, in a strange way. Birch would've given Weichert answers if they were his to give, and Weichert wanted to believe that a man in a lab with clever machines and tremendous knowledge at his disposal could solve any problem. I almost wished Birch would make something up or tell Weichert the things he'd told me, if only to kill the argument and buy some quiet. Instead, the shouting carried on and on— until I'd had enough of it. That's when I stepped between them and slammed my coffee mug on the hard countertop, hard enough to slosh out a splash of coffee and crack the pale ceramic.

"Shut up, both of you," I said. "Shut the hell up."

I spoke with the tone of voice I'd once relied on to send terrified bank employees and their customers into fits of trembling before I even drew my weapon. Birch and Weichert listened.

"It's real simple," I told them. "Two of you standing here hashing words with each other gets no one anywhere. No agreement is gonna come from this. Hear me? You want to keep people alive? You want to know what's going on down in Baxton, why the dead are marching south, what it is that's keeping them on their feet? Go to the damn source. Go to Deadtown. Go and see for yourself."

Damn me and my big, dumb mouth.

After the shock faded from Birch and Weichert's faces, I saw in their eyes they agreed. They'd already made their decision: We had to go. I'd spoken without thinking, and I couldn't back down from my words. From down in the recesses of my mind, animal laughter bubbled up, high-pitched and shrill, only it wasn't laughter but the cackling bark of my hated, constant companion, that savvy fucker who knew the day I was fated to die but would never tell me. I wouldn't ever be free of the jackal till I was free of the world.

TWELVE

That night I tried to convince Della that going to Baxton would be a good chance to scout the lay of the land between Camp Cady and Lohatchie, that I'd go, come back, and then we'd sneak ourselves away for good. Guess I wanted to convince myself too. Della said nothing for a long time then she asked to go with me. We both knew Weichert wouldn't allow it, and I knew she didn't really want to leave the compound without Christopher, but I loved her for saying it.

I told her to stay and get things ready for our departure. Christopher grew stronger every day, and I saw how it made sense for him to come with us, another set of good hands, another pair of sharp eyes. Though I didn't say it to Della, Christopher would help keep her mind off the horror all around us. She needed to take care of him and make sure he gathered his strength for the journey. We chewed over the argument until we had nothing left to say, and then we spent the small, black hours of the night cocooned in our room, wrapped tightly together. Della held onto me like she needed to imprint the sensation of my body against hers, trapping the heat and pulse of my life in all her senses. We fell asleep entangled, glued together with sweat, but Della woke before the sun rose and slipped away without waking me. She didn't want to say goodbye, and I didn't go looking for her. That way it felt like any other day. In case I didn't make it back, I left the spare car keys hidden where I knew she'd find them, inside a little box she used to keep her odds and ends, and then I went to meet Weichert at the greenhouse.

The sheriff had gathered a dozen men, including me, him, and Birch, to make the trip. Our plan was to take three jeeps down the highway as near to Baxton as was safe then hike across the open wilderness and come at the town from the northeast to avoid the dead line. By the time I finished packing and got to the greenhouse, Weichert and his group were ready to go and waiting on me and Birch.

"Nice of you to join us," he said.

"Where's Birch?" I asked.

"Downstairs getting some equipment."

Morning spread through the trees, telegraphing the sweltering day ahead of us, but I was grateful to see clear sky in every direction. Weichert's men milled around, unhappy and jittery. I didn't hold a case of nerves against them. No one, including me, wanted to make this trip.

"What do you think we'll find down there?" I asked Weichert.

"Bunch of stinking, rotting dead people," he said. "Doing what stinking, rotting dead people do. If we're lucky, we'll see why they're doing it and how we can stop the bastards."

"What if there is no *why*?" I said. "What if it's just one of those things that *is*, you know? No reason, no logic, only nature."

Weichert turned to me with a stony glare. "You're talking Birch's brand of superstitious bullshit. There's a reason. There has to be a reason. That's how the world works. There's a reason for everything."

Birch appeared, pulling an oversized backpack across his shoulders as he exited the greenhouse. He paused to straighten it then spat a wad of phlegm into the dirt.

"You need to check your makeup again or you ready to go now, princess?" Weichert asked.

"Fuck you, Tom," Birch said, with the kind of cheer he might've used to say *good morning*. "If you're feeling like an eager beaver, you can go on ahead without me. I'll catch up after I finish my coffee and the morning paper."

Weichert shook his head, ignoring the laughter that rippled through his men. He stalked up the trail to the parking lot. The others followed in a loose group. Birch and I fell in at the rear. As we left the clearing behind and stepped onto the narrow trail, a distant bird cawed, a lingering, porcelain sound like a lonely dirge echoing under a vaulted ceiling. We planned to be gone three, four days tops, but I wondered if I would ever see Camp Cady or Della again.

THIRTEEN

We covered thirty-five miles that day, traveling the desolate road out of Camp Cady and through the deserted town, picking up the highway then leaving it behind two exits above the one for Baxton. Or "Deadtown," as everyone called it since Birch's pet name for the place stuck. It was slow going once we left the near stretches where Weichert's men had cleared away old wrecks and dead cars. We encountered fewer dead as we headed south but the road worsened, clogged with massive jams of immobilized cars crammed together like racers waiting for a start flag that would never fly. We passed the remnants of old accidents, too, moments of violent, kinetic chaos preserved in 3-D freeze frames. Corpses occupied many of the wrecks, the remains of folks trapped in bent or crushed cars who died where they sat. Chewed-up arms and half-eaten faces hung out of broken windows. Some hunched behind broken steering wheels or under caved in roofs or framed by shattered glass webs. They stirred as we passed, tried to wiggle loose to get at the fresh meat. We gave them a wide berth and kept moving.

Where the road turned impassable, we drove along the shoulders, and a couple times we forced a path, eight or nine of us straining and pushing to clear cars off the pavement while the others kept watch. Traveling back roads brought little improvement, but it was easier to get around things with open fields, parking lots, and lawns alongside the road. We stopped fifteen miles away from Baxton, and there, with the sun hanging low, we made camp at an abandoned lumberyard. We pulled the trucks into an old warehouse, closed up the place as best we could, and settled in for the night amidst the smell of old wood. With dusk barely behind us, we collapsed, exhausted. In the morning we'd hike across back roads, fields, and rough ground, following a man named Grant, who knew a route to Deadtown that would keep us off the main streets.

Birch and I crashed in a corner, apart from the others. Birch frightened some of them, and none of them much liked him. A few had been lobbing hostile remarks toward me and Birch throughout the day, blaming us for getting their sorry asses dragged along on the expedition. Way I saw it, as long as Birch and I were right there with them to do the dirty work, they could shove their complaints where the sun don't shine. But imagine telling that to a gang of nervous armed men who disagree, and that's why Birch and I kept to ourselves.

Sometime after midnight, Birch shook me awake. I shot upright and reached for my gun, settling down only when I felt his hand pushing on my chest and saw his haunted face staring at me from the dimness. He sat cross-legged atop his rumpled sleeping bag, his eyes two pale smudges in the gloom. The smell of stale sawdust and forgotten oak and pine filled my nose.

"Shit, you scared the hell out of me," I whispered. "What is it, goddamn it?"

"Keep your voice down." Birch touched a finger to his lips and nodded in the direction of the three men on guard outside while we slept. His nylon sleeping bag whispered under him. "I got a bad feeling about Baxton."

"Hundred thousand or more walking dead hanging out there? So do I," I told him. "You woke me up to tell me that?"

Birch slid up against the wall and leaned back. "No."

"Then what?"

"Remember I told you about my dreams?"

"Yeah."

"I had one. It woke me up," he said. "They used to hit me once a week, or so, but lately I've been having them two or three times a night some nights. Wake up screaming and sweating bullets most times."

"They're only nightmares," I told him.

"It'd be nice if you were right." Birch yawned and rubbed his eyes. "What we'll find in Baxton, well, I think we're not going to like it. In fact, I got such a black fog over my thoughts right now, I'd bet you most of us won't leave Deadtown alive."

"Should we turn back?"

"No," he said. "That's the screwy part. I think we're doing the right thing going there, but I'm sure it's going to get ugly."

"Shit, man, what'd you dream tonight?"

"It's not what I dreamt so much as it is how I felt dreaming it," he said. "I was standing in the heart of a gray desert like the surface of the moon, thick dust all around me but clear air. I gazed up at a night brimming with stars, more than I'd ever seen in my life, and then one-by-one they winked out, going dark. I thought how each one might be a sun, and how maybe their worlds froze or flash-burned to ash, everything on them dying in an instant as their star exploded or went dead and black. I wondered how long before our sun burned out. But then the stars changed, became an infinite number of eyes, looking down from the abyss of space. As each one blinked, it vanished. I felt something drawing closer from behind them, a kind of raw energy, vast but lacking purpose. Like the fury of a nuclear bomb when that smoking, glowing dome of destruction goes on spreading, eating up everything in its path with light and fire and wind—except this was the opposite of heat and light. Behind me, someone laughed. It echoed through the air. Then I woke up."

"Damn. You had that one before?"

"No. Not exactly. Something similar with the stars and the eyes and blood once, but never a thing coming out of the darkness. Never felt anything like it before. Felt like a waterfall of pure hate. Mostly I dream about the dead, that they're all around me, going about business as usual as if they hadn't died.

Then they realize I'm alive, and it's like that scene out of *Invasion of the Body Snatchers* when all the pod people shriek at the real people. Remember that? Screw me. I watched too many horror movies growing up. Stuff gets all wound up in your subconscious and comes farting back out when you least expect it."

"Guess so," I said.

Quiet seconds ticked by, marked only by the sounds of men snoring or shifting in their sleep and the creaks of tired boards as the warehouse swayed in the stiff wind. A howling gust kicked up and sent the nearby trees rustling with a noise like rain pattering down. Our guards passed by outside. Their feet crunched the earth.

"I had a dream like that one time," I said. "Everyone in the world was dead except me. Probably a lot of people dreaming that dream. Probably hard not to."

"You might be right," Birch said. "Except sometimes there's someone on the other end of my dreams."

"How's that?"

"Someone sends them to me. He watches me through them. Maybe he's watching all of us now."

"C'mon, you serious?"

"It's someone I know. I'm not sure who." Birch shut his eyes for a moment. "It's someone I killed."

I knew Birch's background, knew he'd almost certainly done violence in the past, so what he said shouldn't have surprised me—but it did.

Birch rubbed his hands together. "It's not a guilty conscience, and I'm not losing my mind. I met him in person before I came to Camp Cady. He fucked me over as bad as he could, did some very nasty things to the people with me, to a woman I loved, and he's been lingering on the edge of my thoughts ever since. He fades in and out, but he's been there almost since the dead plague began. Worst part is he's dead."

Birch studied my face, waited for my reaction.

"How the hell is that possible?" I said.

"I got some ideas," Birch shrugged. "Told you there was more to this than I can explain. There's no question he's dead, but he's no dumb corpse. He has power. He can..." Birch hesitated. "If I tell you this, it stays between you and me. Understand?"

I nodded and mimed zipping my lips shut.

"He can put the dead down with a touch," Birch told me. "No idea how he does it. It's like magic, like he blesses them, and then—it's over, they don't move anymore. I watched him walk through a field after a battle between the living and the dead, and he was putting the broken and crippled corpses to peace. He touched their eyes, and their bodies stopped moving. He did it even to limbs that were no longer attached. And he can travel anywhere he wants. Now he's playing cat-and-mouse with me again."

I opened my mouth to tell Birch how crazy he sounded but then stopped when I thought of the jackal hovering over my shoulder. My longtime companion, who came and went and loved to stand by my side, laughing whenever my chips were down—and as real to me as anything else in life. Maybe Birch and I had more in common than I'd realized.

"You think we could learn how he does that to the dead?"

"No. I think it's something beyond the living. That's why I've kept it a secret. If Weichert found out, he'd think I was a lunatic or he'd never stop hounding me about figuring it out," Birch said. "Remember this and everything I told you, everything we talked about, okay? It's important. Someone needs to keep it alive. The other men will follow Weichert, even the ones who can think for themselves, because when push comes to shove security, company, and what's safe and expedient will win out over what's hard and best. Except you're not built that way. You've got a chance of surviving the long haul. I know he doesn't mean to, but Weichert's going to get a lot of people killed. Not his fault, really. The world changed; he didn't. He's done his best, but it's inevitable. I feel it coming. Maybe you can save some folks, maybe not. Stupid, fucking thing to come waltzing down here into the middle of a town full of walking corpses. Kicker is, though, you're absolutely right. It's the only way to find out what's going on."

"Well, I hope you're dead wrong," I said. "I'd like us all to get back to Camp Cady to put whatever we learn to good use."

Birch didn't register my words.

"Think about this," he said. "When was the last time you got sick? When was the last time you met someone who was sick?

Since the dead rose up, you hear about anyone dying from AIDS or cancer or diabetes or pneumonia? No. Only accidents, infections, gunshots, and being killed by the dead or each other."

"I knew a guy had the flu or something," I said. "Killed him and he became a wormfeeder, but that was weeks ago."

"Hunh," Birch said. "Exception that proves the rule, I suppose. Back at Vanguard I had a corpse that didn't rise—rotted out like it was supposed to. Still can't figure that one out."

"What are you getting at?"

"The new tests I ran compared living cells with dead ones," Birch said. "I started with my own then moved onto samples from some of the others around camp. Told them I was using live cells to find a cure."

"That's not what you were doing?"

"It was a new path to follow," he said. "Bottom line is you do everything you can to keep from getting hurt tomorrow, all right? If I die here someone has to bear the truth forward. Understand me? Maybe it's a small thing but it matters. Someone should live to tell whoever's left alive how important living is now. You know where all my work is. You can figure out enough of it to make it useful. You're smarter than you think."

"Man, no matter how smart you think I am, I don't understand a quarter of what you scribble down. I don't know what to tell anyone, and even if I did, who the hell is there to listen? So hit me with the plain English, and tell me what you're talking about."

"All right." Birch took a deep breath then let it out. "Time hasn't slowed down only for the cells of the dead but for the living, too. Aging, disease, deterioration, all of it has slowed to a crawl. Not for everyone, maybe, but for most folks. We heal at a normal rate, which has me puzzled, and we can still die as we saw the other day. But barring violence, mishap, or suicide, keep yourself intact, and you might live forever."

"You're fucking crazy. Anyone ever tell you that?"

"First thing I say to myself every morning, but being crazy doesn't make me wrong."

"You tell me this shit now?"

"I want to make sure you're careful tomorrow. Don't do anything stupid. Don't be a hero," Birch said. "I never told you but some of the stuff that's come to pass these last few months, that's stuff I dreamt ahead of time. The people I lost, I dreamt that before it happened. I knew I'd be leaving Camp Cady on an expedition like this. I knew a man like you'd be part of it. If I'm right you've got a bigger part to play in what's happening than you realize. I got a bad feeling about myself for what's coming tomorrow. I think the dead see something inside us we can't see ourselves, like they're passing judgment on our sins. I've done a lot of bad shit in my life, you know? Ah, fuck it. I'm nothing but a 'mad scientist.' Go get me a lab coat and a Tor Johnson look-alike, while I practice my hysterical laughter. Anyway, you play it safe tomorrow, so you can go back and tell them what they need to hear. Tell them about my dreams."

"I haven't been inside your head. I haven't dreamt your dreams."

"Yeah, well, I got a feeling you might." Birch lowered himself into the shadows and drifted toward slumber. "Get some sleep, now. You'll need it."

"Fuck you, how am I gonna sleep after that?"

Birch didn't answer. He only commenced snoring.

I closed my eyes, but too many thoughts spun through my mind. Maybe the living and the dead shared some deeper connection than that of predator and prey. Maybe living people still had a shot at a future. I wondered what Della was doing— lying awake in our bed, thinking of me, or glancing out the window at the high quarter moon in the misty sky and listening to the murmur of the woods, I hoped. I tried to summon her face in my memory, but Birch's words consumed me. I considered waking him up and making him talk, but he never said more than his piece. So I lay awake, running scenarios through my head, looking for the single perfect backup plan to guarantee I made it back to Della in one piece and still breathing.

I came up empty.

Not many situations I couldn't find a way to control or manipulate, but this was too big and chaotic, too much un-known, and I only hoped to hell I could roll with whatever punches came in Deadtown.

Later the sun rose and probed the cracks in the walls with blades of dusty light. A strange sensation came on the morning air like an electric fog on my skin, and I thought of the blind energy Birch had described. It made me despondent, made me want to go out and smash something, hurt someone, find all the wormfeeders and hack away at them until my muscles grew too weak to lift a blade. I wanted it all over and done with. I wanted nothing more to do with any of it.

I toyed with the idea of slipping out before the others woke up, going back for Della, and leaving this all behind. But I couldn't. I had to face the fact that part of me wanted to be here, wanted to know. All that had happened, all that I'd seen, everything stretched out ahead of me with Della at my side compelled me to stick it out. Running, hiding, and hoping the dead never caught up or caught us off guard would only ever take us so far, and the time would come when there'd be nothing to do but make a stand.

That's how life goes.

And it's always better to know what you're standing against.

I got up and walked out into the damp yard to take a leak. If I had to meet the coming darkness head on and hold my ground in the face of Birch's nightmare, I wanted to be prepared. If what Birch said about the living was true then everything I'd ever done and said in the name of immediacy, every stolen, breathless moment of passion that had ever fueled me seemed now to amount to little more than a hot puddle of piss. Above the trees, the apricot sky lightened. I finished and walked away.

The day began, and I felt like I used to on the morning of a bank job.

A cold calm settled over me.

FOURTEEN

The dead came for us on the outskirts of Baxton. They poured from every street and alley, every front porch and storefront, a gushing stream of lifeless flesh wrapped in a ripe miasma of putrescence. Rot and dry sores blemished their mottled gray flesh. Their tattered clothes crinkled and flaked with matted dirt and crusted bodily fluids. They looked fake in the direct daylight, like movie props or animatronic amusement park monsters. Remnants of life clung to them in bits of jewelry and identification badges, in shredded uniforms and the ruins of once-fine suits, in T-shirts emblazoned with rock band logos and bicycle shorts that sagged over withered flesh. Yet all their faces bore the same hungry, hollow-eyed, thoughtless death mask. Greedy mouths hung wide on broken jaws. Eager hands grasped with awkward, splintered fingers, gesturing for more, always more, telegraphing their lust for warm flesh. Their dead eyes stared at us, popping open from every part of them, gelid and white in the sun's brightness.

Weichert shouted.

Everyone heeled around and started to run back the way we'd come only to stop short a moment later.

The dead spilled out from the spaces behind us, too, on all sides of us, clogging the road and drawing into a circle that tightened with every shaky step they took. A billowy cloud crossed the sun, throwing down a shadow like the fist of heaven rising to smash us.

We opened fire, throwing round after round into the crowd of lifeless meat, but the dead only shuffled closer. We tightened together, a dozen men paralyzed at the center of a lonely intersection on the cusp of a town that had once been for the living but now stood less hospitable to us than a desert on Mars. Everywhere I looked I saw empty eye sockets on ravaged faces, the eternal grins of skulls stripped of flesh, the sheen of organs bloated with decomposition. Words I'd said to Birch the first week we met came back to me, and I knew I'd been right: This world existed for the dead now. At best the living were feedstock, and at worst, intruders, an infection, an invasive species.

The dead must have known we were coming, maybe through Birch's connection with the mysterious dead man who haunted him. They had laid a trap that left us nowhere to run, no way to fight back. We'd been wading through their stink all morning, listening to their distant, mournful chatter, but that was no less than we expected on the approach to Deadtown. Now, ineffective gunshots popped all around us, but neither Birch nor I drew our weapons. No point. The dread in Birch's eyes told me that some part of his premonition had already come true.

An explosion ripped the air then.

An abrupt gust of heat and a bone-jarring concussion knocked me to my knees. A line opened in the wall of the dead. Men rushed past me, through the thin smoke, to reach it. Someone had thrown a bomb into the mob. I guessed Weichert must've been holding out on us when it came to munitions, and I prayed he had another dozen of whatever the hell he'd used.

I jumped to my feet and Birch and I hauled ass with the others. We ran farther into town, deeper into the masses of the dead, the only direction we could go. Pavement underfoot gave way to grass, grass to dirt and then gravel as we rounded the corner of an auto garage and turned toward a high, chain-link fence in the distance. Behind it across an open field stood a towering water tank, its lofty catwalk accessible only by a single staircase winding up around one of its support columns.

Wormfeeders swept in from all sides, closing ranks like a giant, arthritic hand. Two of our party, Coogan and Daniels, stumbled and screamed. It happened so fast, we couldn't help them. Their bodies twisted as gray arms lifted them, and then they crowd-surfed a tide of clutching, dead fingers, kicking hard and wailing for help. The rest of us kept running. The dead drew so close, an inconceivable number of them. Stopping—even slowing for half a second—would equal suicide. I glimpsed splashes of red as the dead split open Coogan's or Daniel's skin like orange rind, and then the men disappeared beneath a patchwork of rotting bodies.

Three more men—Janson, Libby, and Tanner—fell along the way. They fired blast after meaningless blast into the arms of the fetid things swarming over them. After seeing what had happened to Coogan and Daniels, though, they didn't wait to be picked apart. At the absolute point of no return, each one turned his weapon on himself and cheated the final horror of being eaten alive. Made no difference to the dead. They still divvied up the warm bodies like lazy butchers.

The forward men were scrambling up the fence now, flipping themselves over, and dropping to the clear ground beyond it. Birch and I pumped our legs harder, driven by the cold wave of death tickling our asses. At the fence Weichert shouted for everyone to hustle as he shoved his men up and over then waved like a lunatic for me and Birch to pick up the pace. We did. Our fingers wrapped around rough aluminum and our feet left the ground. Chain link rattled and shook. A sudden weight struck below us. I grabbed for my gun before I realized it was Weichert bringing up the rear. I climbed faster as he closed on me. Weichert, Birch, and I—we all hit the top rail of the ten-foot fence as the dead slammed into the mesh and jolted the whole structure. My fingers slipped loose, but then I was over, the last to clear the fence. Tumbling then slamming against hard ground. Rolling, crawling, scraping to get back on my feet. No question the weight of the dead would bring the fence down; it was only a matter of whether or not we'd reach the water tank ladder before that happened. We had nowhere else to run.

Seven of us had survived the gauntlet. Four were already out of sight overhead, climbing higher and higher toward the catwalk. Again Weichert brought up the rear. I felt an unexpected burst of gratitude and admiration for the sheriff. As much of a hardcase as he was, he was no coward holding onto his authority like a crutch, but a granite-minded man doing what he believed necessary. He was looking out for every man still alive. Birch and I mounted the narrow metal risers. Weichert followed. We were twenty feet up when the fence folded like cardboard under the press of the dead. A swarm of black figures rambled over it, piling up a jumble of flailing corpses as the frontrunners toppled into the tangle of aluminum poles, chain link, and cold flesh. Their clumsiness bought us precious seconds, enough for the men up top to find positions and start shooting the first wormfeeders to reach the stairs. In their excitement to catch us, the ranks surged forward, mashing their fallen into the ground. I pounded the last steps upward, hit the catwalk, turned back, and pulled Weichert up the rest of the way.

All around the base of the tower the wormfeeders churned in a festering, unbroken wave of dead flesh that blanketed the earth. They filled every street and open space, every stretch of ground, stood on every rooftop, every car and truck, and way off in the distance at the limit of our sight, more ambled into the crowd. The noise of them, and the buzzing and clicking of the bugs that came with them could've drowned out the roar of the ocean on a stormy day. I'd never even seen so many living people in one place and of one mind, let alone such hordes of the dead. Estimates of a hundred thousand at Baxton were pitiful. Had to be a half a million. Had to be more. At least that's what it looked like, and I thought, *they must have started gathering here the day the dead plague began.*

Round after round snapped through the air as Weichert and the others dropped a shower of lead to cover the stairs. It didn't take much for good shots to tip a womrfeeder off balance. They always stood up again, yeah, but you could knock them right back down. We'd be safe as long as our ammo held out, which wouldn't be long at the rate of fire it took to keep the stairs clear. Then the dead would climb up to us and force us to fight hand-to-hand.

Birch grabbed my arm and pointed to the center of Deadtown. "Look."

A red light shone bright despite the late morning sun. It rose from the town's distant avenues.

"It's coming this way," Birch said.

The brightness shimmered as it crept through the low canyons of the Deadtown streets.

"Is that fire?" I asked.

Birch shrugged and then called Weichert to come look. The sheriff's face kind of twitched when he saw the glow, and he swore under his breath.

"You got any more of whatever it was you blew up back there?" I asked him.

"One," he said, lifting the edge of his jacket to reveal a hand grenade clipped to his belt. "Scavenged them after that army troop passed us by months back. Wish I had a hundred more. Figure all this one is good for is taking along as many of these scarecrows as I can when I go."

A volley of shots crackled.

The guns fell silent.

I feared everyone had run out of ammunition but they were only waiting for the next wormfeeder to hit the stairs—except the corpses had given up. A smashed pile of them lay wriggling in the shadow of the tower. None of the others approached. They stood still in the soft wind, their heads craned upward in our direction, and everywhere in their soft gray flesh I saw eyes. They stared out from dry blisters and scabby excavations, from cracks in smashed skulls, from dangling stumps of broken fingers, from black gashes in dead skin, from arms, legs, necks, torsos, and shoulders. One wormfeeder missing its lower jaw unfurled a swollen, rotting tongue, and an eye prodded from its tip.

"Would someone tell me already what the fuck is this crazy shit with all the eyes?" Weichert shouted. He slammed the heel of his hand against the steel guardrail. "Dammit, shit, and hell!"

"Language, Sheriff," I said. "When we get back to Camp Cady, you'll be doing time in the swear jar."

Weichert heeled around and tried to glare at me, but a grin cracked his face. He couldn't dampen his laughter. He doubled over as he let loose big-voiced guffaws. Some of the others laughed with him, letting off a little of their tension; the rest—tear-streaked and coated with sweat—gaped at Weichert like he'd lost his mind.

"Hell, that's a good one," Weichert said, when his laughter faded. "Get back to Camp Cady. Heh. Yeah, right. Then I'll open an ice cream shop and retire. Son of bitch, that tickles my funny bone. I should be angry as hell at you, Mr. Cornell, for suggesting we come down here, but never in a million years would I have imagined this many dead could be in one place. Forget the damn swear jar, because we are well and truly fucked. What the hell are we going to do now?"

"We wait," Birch said.

"For what?" Weichert asked.

Birch pointed to the red light moving through town. "That," he said. "We came here looking for answers. I think they're coming to us."

We watched the red glow creep our way, painting the streets with a pale pink luminescence as it came. The dead crowds let it pass, rippling like confetti making way for the wind. It reached the main road beneath the tower and then emerged from behind a house on the corner. It came from a gaunt dead man, his flesh scaled with modest decay, wearing only a pair of tattered blue jeans and dirty boots. The red light radiated from his body. He crossed the street then the field and then ambled over the fallen chain link fence. He stood below us, looking up—and all the dead turned with him, mimicking his gaze like an army of robots, turning thousands of corpse faces toward us, and with them the countless pallid specks of eyes peering. The sight reminded me of the stars from Birch's dream.

The Red Man raised a hand, flashed us a grim smile, and then waved a two-fingered peace symbol.

He started up the stairs.

Weapons ready, we watched him climb. His aura faded until it blinked out altogether when he crested the last step onto the catwalk and faced us. His skin looked pasted onto his bones, etched into the spaces between his ribs, glued to muscle and tendon, and ligament. Two black pits scarred his face—one above his left eye, the other through his right cheek. I looked for the telltale rise and fall of his chest, but he stood as still as the dead.

"Welcome to Deadtown," he said. "Been expecting you."

His voice rattled like a rat scratching inside a metal pipe; it rolled and crackled like his teeth were falling out and rattling around his mouth; it popped and sizzled like frying meat; it escaped him like coffin dust floating from an unearthed grave. Every syllable he spoke cut like razors.

"Stay where you are," Weichert said. "Don't come any closer."

We readied our weapons.

Birch grabbed my arm hard enough to hurt. His face turned pure white, and he struggled for words and air, trying to speak. Then a gunshot drowned out whatever he wanted to say. One of the men, Owens, had shot the Red Man, and now the man looked down at his chest, fingering a dry, fresh wound to the left of his sternum. The bullet had passed through him as if he were paper. Too fast for any of us to react, the Red Man grabbed Owens and seized his gun. He tossed the weapon aside; it skittered along the catwalk before it dropped over the edge. Then, lifting Owens by the waist, the Red Man raised him up and hurled him over the railing. Owens screamed as he plummeted into the hungry horde below us. As they dug into him, the sounds of his flesh tearing and his joints snapping mingled with their hungry groans.

"There's no need for violence. I have business with some of you," the Red Man said. "But if you want to be stupid about it, go ahead. I don't mind adding to my flock. You're all bound there sooner or later. You all died when you came to Deadtown. You died the moment you were born."

"Who the hell are you?" Weichert asked.

The Red Man gestured to the ranks of the dead extended in every direction, and said, "The Lord of the Dead, I am, yet, only a humble shepherd. Witness ye my sheep."

A vein in Weichert's forehead throbbed, and he ground his teeth together. "What's your name?" he said. "How can you be dead and still talk?"

"I'm dead because that man there killed me." The Red Man pointed at Birch. "Why don't you ask him who I am?"

Everyone looked at Birch.

The scientist trembled. Perspiration coated his face. He tightened his hands into fists and pushed ahead of us.

"You're right. I killed you," he said to the Red Man. "*I fucking killed you years ago.* There's no way you can be here. *No damn way.*"

"Now, finally, you remember me," the Red Man said. "Took you long enough. I knew you would sooner or later, especially after all the time I've spent in your head. I thought it would come to you the day I killed your woman, but I don't think you were ready to face the fact that you made me. Could've told you who I am anytime, could've showed you, but I wanted it to come back to you on its own, so it meant more. Do you remember what you said before you shot me?"

Birch swayed and looked as if his knees might buckle. He gripped the rail to steady himself.

The Red Man said, "I remember it."

"How can you be here?" Birch asked. "You died before the dead plague started."

"Did I? Are you sure? How do you know when the dead plague began? Because you saw it on TV and read it on the Internet and they told you what to think? Well, then that must be true. Can't question the good old idiot box. Can't doubt the online chatter. All the talking heads and government officials and people in uniform, all your priests, rabbis, and ministers, all your wizened sages who claim to own the truth. Well, you sure can't doubt them, can you? " The Red Man laughed. "I'm here because I am, and that's all that matters. Do you remember what you said to me or not?"

Birch nodded. "I told you that you weren't God and if you wanted to meet God, here he was in my hand. Then I showed you my gun."

"That's right. Then I said, 'Wishing doesn't make it so.'" The Red Man's voice cracked and grated like a long transmission over a dying radio. "After that you squeezed the trigger so that I could hear your God speak and feel his awful, burning touch."

Napoli, standing behind Birch, slipped his automatic from his pocket, keeping it low and out of sight, planning a shot on the Red Man. It was a mistake, but I had no time to warn him. The Red Man moved too fast. He darted toward the water tank, reached around Birch, and grabbed Napoli's hand. I had never seen one of the dead move so fast. He dragged Napoli in front of everyone then forced his wrist back until the gun barrel touched Napoli's forehead. He squeezed the trigger with his other hand. The shot echoed off the metal tank, a close thunder. The slug pinged into the sky. Napoli's head erupted onto the faded blue paint. The Red Man caught his body as it fell, lifted it up, and threw it down to the hungry dead.

"One more for me and mine," he said. "Who's next?"

No one moved. Birch stared at the glistening splatter on the tank, peppered with bits of bone, hair, and brains, dripping down the side.

"You still think you're God," he said.

The Red Man approached him.

"I came back from the dead, didn't I? I can send you visions. I can control the dead. Aren't those traits of the divine?" The Red Man shook his head. "But you're wrong. I *know* I'm not God. I have you to thank for that. You sent me to where God ought to be—and he wasn't there. The truth is God is dead and gone. He left a long, long time ago. The living taught me that, taught all the dead that, and that's why we've come back: to help you all find your way to the cold light of the universe. Death is the only God there is and death is a perfect God because one day everyone, no matter what they believe or how they live their lives, will become death's eternal disciple."

"Birch," Weichert said.

Birch didn't respond. He gripped the railing, trembling, seemingly unable to turn his eyes away from the Red Man.

"Birch, dammit!" The sheriff raised his voice. "Who is this freak?"

Without loosening his grip on the railing, Birch said, "His name was Darrell Philip Stradley."

"Never heard of him," Weichert said.

"No, you wouldn't have. He's the man who sends me my dreams. I've seen him in them," Birch said. "He killed my friends. He let me live to suffer. And he can kill the dead."

"What the hell are you talking about?" Weichert asked.

Birch said only to me: "He sends me dreams. He watches me. You understand?"

"I'm trying," I said.

"Understand what?" Weichert said. "What do you mean he can kill the dead? How? Make some damn sense already."

"Let me help with that," the Red Man said. "Let me send you all on a little daydream."

The red light flared and shimmered out of the Red Man's body. It emanated from him, enveloped us, and cast the world in a reddish tint, like looking at Christmas lights through blood smeared on a pane of glass. It brightened until it hurt my eyes; it flared with a silent eruption of energy. My skin crawled. My hair stood on end. I felt like I had to piss, like I might throw up, like my skull might crack apart. My mouth dried out. The red light consumed everything but us and the Red Man. Then it flickered and sparked out, leaving us in darkness, my eyes struggling with the gloom of night, under an open sky, outside on a summer night...

FIFTEEN

...in the dank, littered space behind a strip mall convenience store. A sliver of moon hangs over us. The odor of trash rides the breeze. A young man emerges from the store's back door, dragging three big bags of trash behind him. A fat woman in a green-and-white uniform leans out of the open doorway, shouts at him, then slams the door shut. The man pulls the garbage along to a dumpster placed against a chain link fence. Beyond it stand

trees, a slight hill, and then yards and houses, where television lights dance in the windows. One of the bags tears open and spills out the remains of food, wet paper, and other debris. A stink rises from it. The man swears and kicks the broken bag, spilling more trash. He takes the other bags to the dumpster, shoves the lid up then crams them inside.

It's difficult to see, but the resemblance is there: the man is Stradley.

Younger.

Alive.

He kneels to clean the trash spill. Then he coughs and his body jerks like someone pulled on strings tied around his shoulders. His eyes roll back in their sockets, and his head tilts toward the sky. He slips into a trance, his attention turned to the night.

"If you want to know who I am, you need to understand who I was. A minimum wage slave who could barely hold a job on the convenience store night shift," the Red Man says.

I stand in the alley beside the Red Man and Birch. The others stand with us, all of us apart from what's happening, like we've invaded Stradley's dream—or his memories. Blank patches and gray areas hang in mid air, holes in reality. Trees, boxes, litter, and other things come and go or change. I feel solid ground under my feet, but I'm a foot above the earth. Kneeling beside the trash, Stradley's young self shimmers, then separates into two of himself, one a ghostly duplicate of the other. The faded double approaches us.

"I was a big fat failure," he says. There's a gray cast to his face. Light and shadow seep through him. He wipes his garbage-stained hands on the front of his green-and-white work shirt. "I had no friends. My family wanted nothing to do with me. I wasn't even a junkie or a criminal or a head case they could rally around and try to save. I was one hundred percent pure loser. That busted garbage bag I'm cleaning up is full of wilted vegetables from the salad bar and magazines some kid threw up on. That's the smell of no life. You know what I was thinking about while I was doing that? Going home after work to masturbate in front of the TV. That was my goal. Except even that didn't work out for me, because this was the night I finally decided to give in and listen to the damn Voice."

Ghostly Stradley bends over his double and feigns whispering in his ear.

"Yadda, yadda, yadda," he says. "The Voice popped into my head one night, and it wouldn't go away. I ignored it for days, weeks, months but it kept talking, telling me to do things, to say things that I refused to do—until this night. After that bitch boss of mine screamed at me about the damn trash one too many times, I finally agreed. Knee deep in trash and kid vomit, I figured what the hell did I have to lose? If I was going crazy, I may as well enjoy it. And that was the end of this dumb loser."

Stradley kicks his double in the back, knocking him facedown into the spilled garbage. He kicks him again, and the double rolls into a ball. Stradley erupts into a rage, shouting and spitting, kicking and hitting the body until it bleeds and stops moving. His appearance changes, jumps between that of his younger self and the dead Red Man who stands less than three feet away from me. He gives a final kick.

The red light fills my eyes. The world vanishes into it. I feel dizzy and sick, flush with clinging warmth, and when the light dies, I stand with the others in the convenience store stockroom, where young Stradley beats his boss. Their green-and-white uniforms hang torn and disheveled. He slaps her face, shoves her, knocks her into stacks of boxes. He yells at her, calls her a bitch, shouts that he won't take her shit anymore, and if she doesn't like it, he'll do worse, much worse, he promises. Violence ripples off of him like heat. I've seen scenes like this before; he'll kill her if she pushes him. I want to grab him and make him stop, but I'm paralyzed.

"I felt good when I did what the Voice told me to do," the Red Man says. "First thing it said was to beat the shit out of my dumb bitch boss. She never nagged me again. It was easy after that. When I did what the Voice said, people listened to me. They respected me, some of them at least. And I didn't give a fuck about the rest. They feared me, and that was even better."

The Red Man stands beside his younger self, watching himself hit the woman, and every time she flinches or cries out, his dead smile deepens.

"That was a good night," he says.

The red light flashes, filling my gut with nausea, and the Red Man's dream—or whatever the hell he's dragged us into— becomes a red-and-black swirl of violence and chaos. Flashes of his life play out around us. In a smoke-filled nightclub, Stradley beats a man in a corner, both of them moving in jump-cut motions as strobe lights flash around them. A group of people watches, cheering him on. There's a gleam of joy in Stradley's eyes. The red light flashes. Stradley sits on a tall grave marker in a cemetery at night, speaking to a dozen people, many of the same faces from the cheering crowd at the nightclub. Most hold bottles of beer or liquor or plastic cups. Stradley's words mesmerize them. The red light flashes. Stradley leads a group down a dark street. Armed with baseball bats, boards, and pipes, they're hunting one of the women from his crowd of followers. When they find her, she vanishes beneath Stradley's gang, lost in a flurry of striking weapons. The red light flashes, and when it fades this time, I notice the others look as sick as I feel every time it comes and goes. It leaves us pale and wobbly, and the sights of Stradley's life do nothing to soothe us. Now he's in a room with three women, all of them naked, and Stradley goes at them in turn with short bursts of angry thrusting, while a dead man lies in the corner, blood dripping from his cut throat. Again, the red flashes. Stradley speaks to a crowd crammed into the living room of a rundown house, and I see it now, in their expressions, in their body language, how these people don't simply follow Stradley—they idolize him. He has a hold over them. The red light flashes. Stradley stands on the front porch of an old farmhouse, his face matured, all traces of doubt and weakness expunged by confidence and arrogance, by hatred, meanness, and lust. He shouts to a crowd of fifty people or more gathered on the lawn. More come from cars parked on the street, all of them en- rapt by Stradley's words. Standing there with the Red Man is almost like being there, but the sound is muffled, and the scenery is broken and disjointed, and there's a stiffness about the people, a plastic tension in their faces, as if they're afraid to show Stradley any emotion other than joy. Stradley erupts into frenzy. He stamps back and forth along the porch, waves his arms; the crowd cheers. He shouts and points to a man near the middle of the group, and like a single organism, the crowd turns on the man and swallows him with abrupt violence.

"What the hell did you say to them?" I ask.

"Only what they wanted to hear," the Red Man says. "I told them what the Voice told me. I told them they were living their lives all wrong. I showed them how to liberate themselves from the preconceptions and rules that made them miserable. I taught them it was okay to take what they wanted, to enjoy it, to be happy, to put themselves ahead of anyone else, to play by their rules and no one else's. To live...well, kind of like you do, now that I think about it."

"I never lived like this," I say. "I only stole money. I never hurt anyone for no reason. The only man I ever killed was the man who shot my woman."

"And the two sorry bastards standing behind him. Forget about them?"

"No."

The Red Man shrugs. "But so what? Right? You were justified and that makes you better than me, better than the people who followed me? Is that how you see it? I know you tell yourself you live for freedom, but you're a slave to the shitty remains of living society, beholden to an old-fashioned ideal of playing house with your best gal. You've got no concept of what real freedom is or how free you could really be."

"How do you..." I say. "How do you...know about me?"

The Red Man makes guns of his dead fingers and mimes shooting some invisible target. He smiles.

The red light flashes. I'm frozen again, behind the farmhouse where acres of fallow land sprawl. Stradley's people plant it and build rough cottages. The group grows. Many people younger than Stradley arrive as well as some older, but all of them lost, angry, and disillusioned. I see it in how they avoid each other's eyes, in how they throw themselves into their work, and how Stradley electrifies them—like they all want to avoid ever again thinking about where they came from. They worship Stradley, stop and stare at him when he passes, act without hesitation when he speaks. Stradley walks the grounds like a king. At night people sit around bonfires, waiting until he comes, and when he does, brutal revelry breaks out. Wild dancing, and drinking, and fighting, and fucking by the firelight, and Stradley observes it all with approval before he chooses his entertainment for the night. Some nights he picks a man or a woman and tortures them by the bonfire. Other nights he takes a woman or two or more into the shadows and orders them to please him. The red light flashes…

Rows of cages in the woods, half buried in the earth, filled with those who've lost Stradley's favor as well those whom he favors most.

The red light flashes…

People tied high up on trees, naked, left for days without food or water and some of them, it's horrible to realize, are grateful to be there.

The red light flashes…

Someone butchers a body in the light of a bonfire, slicing pieces of it away and passing it around, heated over the flames then devoured by Stradley's followers.

The red light flashes…

Deep in the woods on a sunny morning, Stradley kneels beside a corpse, touches its forehead, and its eyes flutter open, dead white, before its mouth cracks wide and howls.

The red light flashes…

Daylight. Two police officers stand on the farmhouse porch by the front door with a sickly woman propped between them. Two of Stradley's followers greet them from the shadows of the entrance, their faces as bruised and cut as the woman's, but their wounds are older, healed over. The woman tries to go inside, but the cops hold her back, until Stradley emerges from behind his people. He shimmers and sprouts another ghostly double, who walks down the steps to meet me and the others on the front lawn.

"Cops showed up here a lot. Those bastards never paid me the proper respect," he says. "They brought home our strays, the ones who wandered off to the hospital in town when things got too rough for them. Low-dose strychnine poisoning or a few teeth cracked off above the gums. Acid burns or patches of missing skin that wouldn't heal. My true believers bore those burdens like badges of honor, but not the weak ones. It didn't matter. The cops questioned us every time. Not one of my people ever talked, though. They knew how bad it would be for them if they did. And whatever excuse we gave, I had a dozen or more people

ready to back it up, to tell the police the injuries were accidents or self-inflicted."

The red light flashes…

The farm brims with more people than it can handle. Groups have set up camps in the fields where they sleep in tents or under open sky. Some never leave the bonfires. Sick, wounded, tired, naked, filthy, lost, they sleep where they fall when each night's revelry ends.

The red light flashes…

Stradley stores weapons in the barn. Machetes. Pitchforks. Handguns. Shotguns. Semi-automatic rifles. Explosives. Enough for every person living on the farm.

More than enough.

The red light flashes…

Stradley mortifies his flesh with a cat o' nine tails and his faithful follow.

Stradley purges his soul on the flesh of his followers and his faithful follow.

Stradley fasts for a week and his faithful follow.

The red light brightens, dims…

None of Stradley's faithful match his fervor; none attain his heights of transcendence. He enters a trance and floats off the ground. He heals his followers with the touch of his right hand, maims them with his left. He makes the sun and the moon stand still in the sky, and he turns the waters of a stream to blood. He makes the fire dance and spark. A red aura embraces him in a full-body halo. Yet while his power grows, the outside world keeps pressing in. Suspicions never die. The police come around more often. They watch who comes and who goes from the property; and they monitor the bonfires at night. Stradley sees to it that every man and woman on the farm has a gun, plenty of ammunition, and a knife, a machete, or a hatchet. In Stradley's mind, he's already won. The cops won't risk a stand-off, and as long he keeps his people's activities contained to his land and out of sight, there's nothing they can do.

The red light carries us forward…

New faithful arrive, and Stradley takes their money. He holds it, accumulates it, builds a fortune, until he hits the big time the day a manic-depressive millionaire, aging into dementia, rolls up in his limousine. The rich man signs everything he owns over to Stradley and joins the people at the farm. Stradley turns the wealth he's collected toward a stockpile of death: black market nerve gasses and disease specimens. He stows them in the barn, in the woods, in the basement of the house.

The red light flashes...

The men come on a cold, clear night with the lights of their vehicles turned off; they give no warning, no chance for Stradley to arrange a stand-off. FBI agents and local police with special military support swarm onto the farm, cutting the dark with precision and determination, free to kill anyone who resists too much. The operation is a secret; a cover story about a right-wing militia is already floating around the fringes of the media in case things go wrong. The firefight turns heavy fast, casualties on both sides, but more among Stradley's people, whose bodies litter the ground. They run in groups against the intruders, almost mindless, their eyes brimming with rage and a hunger for flesh and blood. They look like the dead, the illusion only broken when one of them falls or dies and doesn't rise. The farm complex burns, the cottages, shacks, and tents go up fast, engulfed in flames carried by the wind. Columns of smoke rise toward the stars.

The red light flashes...

Now Birch stands before us.

Younger, fitter, his hair darker, and a hard light in his eyes. A trained killer's stare. He wears a black uniform devoid of insignia, a belt laden with equipment, and an automatic rifle strapped to his back. He clutches a black forty-five in his hand. He chases Stradley through the farmhouse, into the cellar, where Stradley works at opening a canister of nerve gas, but Birch arrives too fast. He knocks the canister from Stradley's hands and kicks him to the floor.

He shows him his weapon.

They exchange words about God.

The red light flashes...

Three shots: two through Stradley's head, one through his right lung.

The red light...

SIXTEEN

...faded away, dispelled by daylight flooding my eyes.

Fifteen years later Stradley's corpse still bore its fatal wounds.

He touched each one, and I heard the echo of Birch's gunshots in the recesses of my mind. The Red Man laughed. A sick feeling came over me. I clutched my stomach, doubled over, and dry heaved. Weichert and Birch did the same. Lee and Ferring hung their heads over the railing and retched into the air.

When I recovered, I said to Birch, "After fifteen years, he should be rotted away to bones and dust. How the hell did he rise?"

"I don't know," Birch said.

"It's true. I shouldn't be here," the Red Man said, and for that one moment his voice sounded normal, human, and living, as if the last dying scrap of his soul recalled what life had been like and wanted to wish away all the bad things Stradley had done and seen—but that moment passed fast. Then the Red Man's monstrous voice returned. "I learned things after I died. Where I'd been right and wrong in life, what the Voice was trying to tell me, and where it came from. Everything my faithful ever said I did was true. I can still do all those miracles and magicks. The world condemned us for how we lived, but there was holiness in it. And purity, too. Not any polite kind, no, but our pain and deprivation opened our souls. We lived like mad monks in the wilderness, scorning the needs of the flesh, beating our bodies down so that the spirit might thrive, and no one's spirit thrived more than mine. I believed in everything we did. Oh, *how* I *believed*—more than anyone else ever could. I became the saint of sinners, a shaman, a dark bodhisattva, a holy man with the powers of Heaven and Hell in my touch and a direct line to the divine."

The Red Man surveyed the dead gathered in Baxton. A few at the base of the tower still dripped blood from feeding on Owen and Napoli. The Red Man smiled, skeletal and reptilian, like a split in the bottom of the earth.

"Holy men don't rot when they die. Our bodies remain incorrupt. Crack a history book if you don't know what I'm talking about. My assassins buried me in a pauper's grave, where I lay dead as a stone for years, a relic till my body rose and walked again. What I saw in death, what I came back knowing...." The Red Man shook his head as if recalling the awe of his experiences. "Chaotic multitudes of souls swirled around me like grains of sand spinning in a whirlwind. An endless stream of raw energy flowing through the void. A storm of anger, bitterness, and isolation. Billions of dead crying out for the afterlife, for the Word, for anything that might fill their emptiness and tell them what to do—and hearing only silence in reply.

"I found others like me beyond death. Souls who remembered and knew the dead were abandoned. But they were weaker than me. They forgot who they were. Like all the others, they became only whatever it was they'd felt when they died, and for a lot of people—*for so many people*—that was either pure, burning rage at dying or icy fear at what comes next. Those souls wanted only one thing: to *live* again. Sure, a few voices of love and mercy cried out amidst the din, but they were faint. And easily silenced. When the needs of the dead hit a fever pitch, I was there to answer. *We* were there. The saints and the holy men. The magicians, the shamans, and the devils. And speaking with one voice, we said, *'Rise!'* And the dead did listen."

The Red Man's horrible voice faded into the wind.

Then the wind died, stranding us in silence.

Birch hung his head. Weichert panted through gritted teeth. Lee and Ferring clutched their guns, talismans to protect them.

"A God once existed to tend all souls, that much is true," the Red Man said. "But he died, or went away, or we killed him with our perversions, or our indifference, or maybe he abandoned us out of disgust or boredom or because he had better things to do. Who can know the mind of God? Who cares? What matters is what he left behind: nothing. A void to contain the souls of the dead. With nowhere to go and with the help of those of us who hold the secrets of life and death, they turned back to the flesh that once served them. But they found their flesh rotten and decayed and no good to accommodate so many righteous, angry ghosts. Where could the ones whose bodies had burned or disintegrated or been broken beyond recognition go? The ones whose corporeal homes had been pulled apart and divvied up among the living? They could only shelter in what bodies remained, many souls dwelling as one."

The Red Man raised his arms above his head. Smoky, crimson light streamed out of him. His flesh bubbled and coruscated like an infestation of bugs writhed beneath it. A hundred or more bloody seams creased his skin then snapped open with liquid rents that jetted sprays of blood and revealed eyes covering every part of his body. They blinked against the brightness of the sun.

"Many souls dwell in me for my corpse is strong," the Red Man said. "The souls of the dead demand what was once theirs: living flesh."

He grabbed Grant, our guide, by the scalp, tugged him up close, and bit hard into his arm, gnawing, working the joint until the limb popped loose. Weakened, sickened, and shocked, none of us could stop him. Grant didn't fight back, didn't utter a sound, when the Red Man threw him over the railing to the corpses below, keeping back his arm. Blood spilled down the Red Man's mouth and chest as he sucked on the torn limb. Blood ran into the eyes of his flesh.

"The dead came back to...*eat* the living because somehow, some way, we killed God?" I said. "What the hell? What about all you dead sons-of-bitches who lived and died before us? Weren't you the ones who did the killing?"

"Don't believe him," Birch said. "He was insane when he lived. A con man, a pervert, and a megalomaniac. There's more to this, Cornell. I've seen it in my dreams. He's not telling everything. He's not as strong as he thinks. The world isn't done with the living yet."

The Red Man spat a hunk of gristle onto the catwalk. "Shut up, Birch. No one cares what you say. Murderer."

He dipped a finger into the stump of Grant's arm then reached out faster than I could follow and smeared blood onto my forehead. His touch lasted only a moment, but it chased the heat and strength right out of my body. I shuddered. My knees bent, and I nearly fell.

"The dead know no mercy," he told me. "Death to the flesh to free the spirit, death to the spirit to free the flesh."

He crushed his thumb against Birch's forehead the same way, daubing an "X" on his skin, leaving Birch and me leaning against the water tank to keep on our feet. He shoved by us to get at the others. He ripped out Lee's throat. He gutted Ferring and then dropped them on the catwalk. He reached for Weichert, but the sheriff jabbed a knife into an eye on the Red Man's chest. It popped like a blister. The Red Man shrieked, but without pain, without fear; joy filled his voice. He welcomed whatever injury Weichert gave; he ate it up and waited for more. Weichert stabbed another then another. For every eye Weichert blinded, a new one popped open to replace it.

A little energy returned to my body. I felt steadier. I drew my knife from its sheathe on my belt, and then mustering everything I had in me, I crept behind the Red Man, the eyes on his back and shoulders lighting my nerves on fire with their stare. Then I sliced my blade into the side of his neck, dug in, and twisted. I brought the cutting edge down exactly how Birch had showed me, biting into the Red Man's spine. Something snapped. His head drooped. He took two steps then punched Weichert in the chest, sending up a little burst of red light as he cracked bones and slammed the sheriff backward. Then he crushed me against the water tank. A crimson haze filled my eyes, and I thought we might flash away again to another time and place. Then the Red Man let go of me and touched the dry wound at the back of his neck. It glowed for several seconds and when he lifted his fingers, his wound was healed.

He looked at me and shrugged. "You tried."

He hefted Lee's corpse over the railing then caught Ferring, who emptied his gun into the Red Man and kicked to get away. It did no good. The Red Man tossed him over. Weichert caught my attention. His chest heaved as he struggled to breathe. His pale face dripped sweat as he lifted the flap of his coat to show me the grenade still clipped to his belt. I took the hint and nodded.

When the Red Man came for him, Weichert—still choking and gasping for air—spat blood and saliva into the dead man's face. I scrambled away, a sharp pain in my chest telling me I probably had at least one bruised or broken rib, but I ignored it. I grabbed Birch and hurried him toward the far side of the tower.

The grenade blew too soon.

The catwalk bucked and the tower shook. I tumbled into the air, lost my grip on Birch, and came down rough, smashing my face against coarse metal. Iron scraps darted around me, clanging against the catwalk and its railing. A jet spray of water followed and hit my legs, shoving me toward the catwalk edge. The spray surged, and a river gushed from the tank. I grabbed on to the platform, digging my fingers into the sharp grooves of the metal mesh. Water swamped me in a flash flood. It cascaded onto the dead below.

Something jabbed my arm.

Straining, I saw Birch hanging over the side of the catwalk, clutching the edge with one hand, digging into my side with the other.

"Remember my dreams," Birch shouted over the roar of the water. "Remember everything I told you."

I grabbed his hand, but his wet fingers slipped loose and the raging water carried him away. I hollered his name. A flash of red sparkled below me. I closed my eyes and focused on holding tight. It felt like hours that the water flowed, icy, hammering at my legs, filling my ears with thunder, as it pushed and pulled, trying to drag me over the side. The world became a roiling, wet spiral hell-bent on punishing me. My hands ached and cramped. Pain lanced my wrists. The edges of the metal grooves sliced my fingertips. My body teetered on the brink of exhaustion. When I thought I couldn't hold on any longer, when I felt my feet creeping over the catwalk edge and dangling in empty air, the gusher died. The pressure dropped. The flow of water slowed to a feeble stream.

I flopped over on my back and sucked air.

After a while I forced myself to sit up. A gaping hole full of darkness faced me from the ruptured water tank. No sign of Weichert or the Red Man. I looked over the catwalk edge and saw the dead down there scattered and busted up by the fallen water. They wiggled like ants caught in a sudden downpour. An enormous puddle spread out from the tower, and a steady stream of water drops rained from the catwalk. It pattered like ice melting off the edge of a frozen roof.

I sat alone.

I screamed, loud and harsh, straining my voice to its limits, venting my anger to the open sky, shouting my horror and frustration to an indifferent world, until my voice cracked and faltered.

After that my mind blanked for a time.

Metal bit into my back. The dead would come for me sooner or later. I should've gotten up and ran. But I was too washed out to fight half a dozen wormfeeders let alone a hundred thousand. I rolled onto my side and watched the trees on the edge of town dance in the blustery afternoon, wishing I'd been able to keep my last promise to Della.

The jackal sat by my side, licking his paws.

Not laughing now.

Strange as it might sound, I was grateful for his presence. I mistook his silence for sympathy, his restraint for comfort, but I should've known better that no kindness dwelled in him, that the dead world and its scavengers were far from done with me. I think the jackal sat so quietly by my side because the fate he foresaw for me horrified even him. But I didn't think that then. I was only glad not to be by myself. After all, a dying man grasps at whatever lifeline comes within reach.

I blacked out and fell into nothingness.

I dreamed of the red and the black, of voices and stars, of the dead, and swarms of eyes, of a universe whose existence depended what those eyes saw.

When I woke stars glittered in the night sky like ice crystals on a blanket of black, virgin glass. I waited for them to snuff out like they had in Birch's dream, but they kept twinkling. The moans of the dead rose from beneath the tower. I shivered in cold air that turned my sopping clothes to a shroud of ice. I drifted back into unconsciousness.

In the morning, stiff and aching from lying so long on hard metal, shaking from the chill that had seeped into my bones, I opened my eyes and crept to the edge of the catwalk. Every move ignited firecrackers of pain. No sign of Birch or the Red

Man or any of the others. Only the dead remained, holding vigil. I wondered why they hadn't come for me in the night.

I waited an hour, but they ignored me.

"Enough of this shit," I said.

I stood up, limped to the stairs, and descended.

SEVENTEEN

The dead refused to touch me.

When I set foot on the ground I braced for them to rush me, but not one of them did. I walked right up to them, shouted, and cracked one of them in the face with the stock of a shotgun I'd retrieved from the mud.

Nothing.

Gangly and frail like scarecrows, dappled with black stains of rot, they watched me. Something about Weichert's preferred name for them seemed right to me then.

Scarecrows.

"What the fuck's wrong with you?" I shouted.

Silent eyes regarded me.

To my left stood a dead man in a brown courier's uniform, his face mashed beyond recognition. From a muddle of crusted wounds peered stark, rheumy eyes. I put my shotgun in his face and blew his head off.

Nothing.

He only fell over and crawled away, headless, through the mud.

The rest of the wormfeeders—the *scarecrows* did nothing.

Like I didn't even exist.

Wherever I walked, the dead let me pass.

Down among them the stench of decay became almost suffocating, and to my horror I realized I'd gotten a little bit used to it. I tore off a patch of my shirt and tied it over my mouth and nose to take the edge off the stink. I couldn't stop their groaning and gurgling. I crossed the muddy field, passed the auto shop, headed toward the street where the dead had ambushed us yesterday, and found the road out of town. I passed the crater Weichert's first grenade had left. I moved into the shade of the trees and kept going. As much as I didn't want to, it proved impossible not to stare at the death surrounding me in all its strange and savage glory. Bodies ripped open. Limbs hanging by threads of drying ligaments. Dead faces mottled purple and gray. Eyeless skulls. Organs poking out of flesh split open like old leather. Scraps of metal and wood broken off and still protruding from rotted meat. And always, the eyes. Those damn, dead eyes, tracking me wherever I went.

After a while I stared right back at them.

Trying to ignore them made it worse. Something had shifted around in my mind and changed how I saw them. It rose out of disgust and frustration but settled into anger. I glared at every one of the eyes I saw as I walked through the mob. I flashed them the stare that had earned me the fear and respect of lawmen who'd hunted me and thousands in loose cash from the hands of terrified bankers.

An unexpected thing happened then: those dead, white eyes blinked.

The longer I looked back at them, the more of them that blinked, twitching odd folds of flesh. I stared back at least as good as I got, and a lot of them dropped their gaze to the ground, looked off to the side, or closed up. I stared down the dead. My stride grew more confident. Maybe Birch pegged it, and the world still needed the living. I didn't understand it, didn't see what role other than food we might yet have, but I suspected that the dead did, and that's why they didn't take me. That and because the Red Man had smeared his sign on my forehead.

A hundred yards more and the dead fell behind me. A hundred thousand, a half a million, however many they were, I was leaving them and Deadtown, and the dead let me go. I walked out from their shadow. The road lay open, only the empty earth, and the far horizon, and the path home free and clear ahead of me, and not a dead thing in sight.

I didn't look back.

Not once.

I walked until my legs ached and my body screamed for water, and then I forced myself to keep moving, pushing one foot ahead of the other, grinding for every inch of ground, staggering north until the dark made it impossible to go any farther. With the day's sun a memory I found an office without windows in the back of a grocery store, blocked the door with boxes, and then I slept.

EIGHTEEN

I woke during the night, my body a rolling wave of pain. Three wormfeeders stood over me, swaying like drunks, a rotten stench pouring off them. Maggots crawled over their pitted flesh, and flies buzzed in the dregs of their clothing. One wore a hunter's cap, the second a police hat, and the third was bald with the top of his skull caved in like a soft-boiled egg. The eyes of their bodies glowed in the dimness. I reached for my gun but by the time I brought it around, they'd lost interest and shuffled away.

I leapt up, slammed the door behind them, and then barricaded it with more boxes and office furniture. I sat up for a time, expecting others to come, but nothing stirred in the corridor. I dozed back to sleep, but it brought me no rest. Instead, my mind came alive to visions of a sweeping darkness filled with the eyes of the dead. They rolled on a black wave like flotsam on a stormy ocean. I hunted for safe shelter. A dry, granular rain pelted my skin and peppered me with sooty smears; in the distance a pillar of light lanced into the night. Showers of brightness erupted from it like fireworks. I ran toward it, drawn by the voices coming from its glow—all dead, meaningless voices. I reached the light and saw it came from the light of countless souls ascending out from an infinite field of graves and pouring upward into the sable sky. As each reached the pinnacle of its ascent, it flared and flickered then snuffed out. The flashes of light lit the ruins that surrounded me. The remnants of bright buildings cast long shadows, and enormous, glassy eyes with blue, green, and yellow irises stared up from beneath the ash and soil. I sensed a black line of annihilation crossing the infinite space behind me. Everything it touched withered, and behind it lurked a wicked, faceless will. Malicious. Greedy. Bloated with dread and despair. A brazen, irresistible, hollow with an endless hunger aching to be filled.

I woke up in a cold sweat from my dreams—*Birch's dreams*—and I understood what had been behind the haunted look I'd so often seen in his eyes.

The dream had been as real as anything I'd ever experienced. I felt the presence Birch had described, like something hiding behind a curtain or waiting in the next room. It had reached into my head. I felt the echoes of its touch. Maybe the Red Man. Maybe something else. I shook it off as best I could then relieved myself in the back corner and headed out into the morning.

I needed to find Della and Christopher; it was the only thing I wanted. The Red Man had known we were coming, so I figured he must have known about Camp Cady. The dead line ran so close by, maybe he had used them to spy on us. Maybe he had even sent the dead that had wandered in and attacked us. Anything could've happened at the camp while I was gone. I needed to know that Della and Christopher were all right.

I crept along the back of the grocery store, checking each cluttered aisle I passed. Almost nothing left but junk and spoiled food but hunger drove me to search the debris anyway. I turned up an unopened bag of marshmallows hidden under a pile of dented pots and pans and broken glassware. I tore it open and shoved three into my mouth.

Sweet and fluffy.

Marshmallows never go bad.

Up front past the cash registers, the glass windows were smashed. Something there bumped then crashed.

I shoved the marshmallows into my shirt, grabbed my shotgun, and eased down the produce aisle. A man stumbled through the wreckage of the front entrance. The sun at his back made him a shadow, but he didn't move like the dead.

I wrapped my finger around the trigger. "Something I can help you with, champ?"

Startled, the man jerked forward, stumbled, and fell to his knees, grunting, waving his hands. He inched out of the brightness, and as my eyes adjusted, I recognized Birch. Blood-smeared clothes and wild eyes, his forehead tagged with a daub of blood like the one on me. He looked like he'd aged ten years overnight. I couldn't imagine how he'd survived falling off the water tower. He gestured to his open mouth, spitting, sort of snarling a little. A trickle of blood dribbled over his lips. His tongue was gone.

"Sonofabitch, Birch," I said. "I'm glad you're alive, but what the fuck happened to you?"

I hooked my arm under his and helped him to his feet. We stepped outside into the morning light. It wasn't easy, but Birch made it clear that the Red Man had mutilated him and that the dead had led him here in the night and left him for me to find. There was more to the story, but he didn't have it in him to tell me then. All the time I'd slept on the water tower and hiked away from Deadtown, Birch had been with the Red Man, a man he'd killed, a dead man who was more than a man now. I tried not to think about what else the Red Man might have done to him.

Birch and I traced the remaining path back to our lumber-yard camp and reached it by early afternoon. We took one of the jeeps and drove north. Birch nodded off right away, and I sank into a loneliness deeper than any other I've ever known. We passed the dead along the side of the highway, more now than we'd seen on our way down. Maybe drifting away from Baxton now that all the excitement was over or maybe arriving late to the party. They roamed along the road and picked through wrecked cars for food. Sometimes they turned and chased us, but I hit the gas and let them grow small and vanish in the rearview mirror.

I kept the pedal to the floor whenever I could. The world became a place of streaks and blurs, punctuated by snapshots of scenery when road conditions forced me to slow down. Ruined cars formed a slalom run on some stretches, but no matter how much the jeep jerked and swerved, Birch slept through it. The speedometer needle quivered and the hum of the engine drilled into my head. I rammed some of the dead along the way. They fell beneath the wheels or burst in a mess of viscera that spattered the windshield. I didn't care. I told myself to slow down but I couldn't. No matter how I tried, I couldn't bring myself to ease up. My leg locked tight, my foot hugged the accelerator. My arms stayed riveted to the steering wheel, my back welded to my seat. I couldn't stop before I found Della.

Close to evening I saw an oncoming car across a clear stretch of road, and finally the spell broke.

The other driver noticed us about the same time. Our vehicles screeched to a stop, maybe a quarter mile between us and separated by a grassy ditch between the lanes. None of the dead lingered nearby, but we'd passed half a dozen a couple hundred yards back, and I wasn't happy to be sitting still. I tried to see the other driver, but the setting sun glancing off the car's windshield made it impossible. Then I recognized its familiar shape and blue paint: Mason's car. I prayed that meant what I hoped it did, but in case it didn't I made sure to load the gun I'd found in the jeep before I got out.

A second passed as I approached. Ten. Twenty. Then the driver's side door of the blue car flew open.

Della leapt out.

She raced toward me.

The sight of her destroyed my loneliness.

Della jumped into my arms and wrapped herself around my torso. We clung to each other and kissed, holding on, afraid to separate. We might've stood there forever if Christopher hadn't poked his head out from the passenger side window and shouted, "Get a room, losers."

I laughed.

The sound shocked me.

I hadn't thought I still had it in me, but seeing Della alive, Christopher with her, and the old car that had carried us so far raised my spirits.

"I thought I might never see you again," Della said.

I stroked her hair. "I promised."

"I know." Della tensed. "I wasn't sure Christopher and I would make it."

"What happened?" I said.

"Got bad after Weichert left," she said. "People grabbed weapons and equipment without asking. I acted fast. Christopher and I gathered what we could, packed the car full of food, gear, and guns. No one hassled us. I'd helped most of them, one time or another. Then the dead came, from the direction of the dead line. Dozens poured out of the woods. All our guards we'd sent out to watch came with them. They overran the camp. We took the car and bolted. Some of the others made it out too. They all headed north together. We came south to look for you. Shit, it was like when Mason died. There was nothing left to do but run to stay alive."

"Lucky you found me," I said.

"I had to try." Della's eyes glistened. She wiped them with the back of her hand, and then licked her thumb and scrubbed my forehead with it. "You got some blood on your face. It won't come off."

I eased her hand away. "Worry about it later. I've got a lot to tell you."

We woke Birch and helped him to Mason's car. The jeep would've been a good choice, but with gas so scarce we opted for higher mileage. Besides, Mason's car had served us well and it was already packed. Birch and Christopher squeezed into the back seat with packages and boxes. Della, remembering what I'd told her about Birch's research, had grabbed some of his computers and notebooks, whatever fit into two boxes. Birch stared at it for a long time, and then he dug out a pen and a mostly empty notebook and started scribbling. I slipped behind the wheel with Della riding shotgun and turned the ignition key. The engine growled. I let it idle for a minute, then shut it off and rubbed my eyes.

Della took my hand. "What is it?"

"Where the hell are we going?" I said. "Nothing but the dead in every direction."

"Maybe," Della said. "But one way or another we're going home."

As if the word still meant something.

I was free again. Free of Weichert and his rules, free of giving a shit how other people thought I should live, but I didn't feel free. Instead I felt the Red Man's mark dried onto my skin; I remembered his frigid touch.

I started the engine again, put the car in drive, and roared off south, planning to speed past the Deadtown exit without so much as slowing down. The Red Man had made the other side of death sound a whole lot like life, maybe even worse, maybe even more pointless and punishing, and if that was so, then living forever, like Birch thought we might, didn't sound bad at all. Way I saw it, whatever the Red Man or the dead wanted, none of the living owed them so much as a stray tear or a handful of dirt. I wanted no more to do with any of them. I planned to drive us to Lohatchie, nonstop if I could. But I knew it was a fantasy.

I could never outrun the mark on my head.

And my four-legged friend hadn't abandoned me. The jackal had stayed with me every second since Deadtown. His cackling bark echoed out of every shadow we passed, and his hot breath came on every breeze that rushed by. It tickled the back of my neck. Wouldn't be long, now, I thought, before he let me in on his secrets.

PASSENGERS

ONE

Show the rich bastard what he wants to see, and he'll put the world at your feet.

The voice murmured inside Darrell Philip Stradley's head, unceasing, never silent, his guide and guardian angel since the day he first listened to it. Darrell nodded in agreement as he greeted the black limousine idling at the curb. The engine shut off, pinging as it cooled, and then a chauffeur emerged and rounded the vehicle to open the rear door for his passenger. An old man in a tailored, navy blue suit and a dark red tie leaned on the driver's arm as he rose from the car. His silver hair twitched in the breeze. He clutched a black briefcase by its handle as he swayed and trembled like a sapling in a hurricane.

Stradley watched the man squint with displeasure at the raggedy, overgrown front lawn speckled by tall dandelions and the saw-toothed weeds that sprang from every crack in the walk that led to the farmhouse. The man shaded his eyes from the sun as they took in the many odd faces peering from the house's grimy windows. Other faces spied from the front porch and the sides of the house, from behind untrimmed hedges in the neglected yard, from rows of garbage cans ripe with rotting trash, even from behind an old pickup truck left rusting on four flat tires. Stradley's people, watching his back. He felt their presence and relished it.

The old man's shoulders slumped as he finished his survey. "What a shithole."

Stradley chuckled and reached out to shake the man's hand. "Only a façade, Mr. Nelson, only a façade. You'll like it much better in the Garden, I have no doubt."

Nelson glared at Stradley's hand but didn't shake it.

He doesn't deserve better, doesn't deserve your touch. Show him your fists instead. Bare your teeth. Teach him respect.

Stradley lowered his outstretched hand. "So, how was your trip?"

"I'm here, aren't I?" Nelson coughed, then cupped a handkerchief to his mouth. He spit, then tucked the cloth away in his pocket, but not before exposing a patch of wet crimson. "Now listen, I don't like amusement parks."

"Uh, what's that, sir?"

"You heard me. I'm done with the midway madness. Don't put me in the bumper cars and tell *me* how to drive, understand?"

Stradley eyed Nelson's chauffeur for a clue to the joke, but the man's expression signaled only relief to hand off his burden, as if saying, *He's your problem now, buddy.*

"I'll keep that in mind," Stradley said. "What I meant is we let appearances run down out front to intimidate the locals and keep away prying eyes. The heart of what we do, what we've built, the Garden, is out of sight of the road, of course, but no point making outsiders feel welcome, right? So, you go ahead and drive your bumper car any way you want."

"What the hell are you talking about? Didn't I just tell you I hate amusement parks? Get the wax out of your ears, boyo. Quit pissing away my time, and what say we get to business?"

"I'd say you read my mind."

Stradley reached to help Nelson with his briefcase. The old man swatted his hand away.

"I'm not an invalid, dammit. You'll get *this* when I give it to you."

"Of course. Whatever you say, sir."

Nelson tottered along behind Stradley, taking his time on the steps to the front porch. As Stradley opened the front door for him, the limo growled, and its tires crunched grit as it rolled away. The two men walked to a back room where a picture window framed a view of the farmland that sprawled behind it. Five hundred acres of Central Florida far from the reach of strip malls and beaches. From an unseen fire beyond the soft hills and brush rose a lonely tendril of smoke. A trail wound toward it, past makeshift huts and sheds of corrugated steel, vinyl tarps, and wood and drywall scraps that hinted at more buildings out beyond the tree line. Nelson eased himself into an old leather, high-backed chair and propped the briefcase on his knees. He stared out the window. His jaw loosened, and his mouth drooped at an awkward, aimless tilt.

"I can feel it," the old man whispered.

Stradley grinned. "Good, that's good."

Let him soak in the energy. Let him take a taste. Bait this bastard and then set the hook.

Stradley, his attention fixated on the briefcase, sat in a chair beside Nelson.

Faces appeared at the window. Pallid onlookers gaped at the visitor. Bruises and scars blemished many of them, some wounds gleaming with fresh blood or wet scabs, a few with hair pulled out and blood matted in what remained. Nelson grimaced, but then looked past them at the smoke rising from a fire that seemed to burn in his honor. Without taking his gaze from it, he said, "You greedy creep. You're more interested in what's in my briefcase than anything else."

"I'm most interested in what's in here." Stradley tapped his chest above his heart. "And what's up there." He gestured generically toward the sky. "What you have in that case is a means to an end, nothing more. I'll get where I'm going one way or another, but your help will sure get me there faster."

"I don't give a dog's dump about your ends and means," Nelson said. "I'm dying, you heartless fucker. *Dying.* I want to know where we go after we die. You say you can show me—*really* show me? Then do it so I can die in peace. Then this and much more is all yours."

Nelson popped the clasps on the briefcase and raised the lid to exhibit tight stacks of hundred-dollar bills packed solid inside. A letter-size manila envelope lay atop them.

Every one of those money packets buys a dozen deaths.

"A dozen deaths," Stradley said under his breath.

"Huh, what's that?" Nelson said.

"Just a little prayer of hope."

Faces gathered at the room's entrance. Half a dozen more at the back door. Dirty, torn clothes and bruised, scabby flesh. They eyed the old man and the money with flat curiosity.

"Five million, as agreed."

"Bless you for it, Mr. Nelson."

"Shove your blessing up your ass, Stradley. I'm not here for that. *Show me.* Understand? I don't 'pays my money and takes my chances' anymore. I don't watch the pretty lady while you pick my pocket clean. I buy results. I didn't survive six decades in business gambling with my resources. Dammit, if I can't buy doctors who can save me, who can even relieve my pain and depression, then I want to know what's waiting for me."

"I hear you, Mr. Nelson. You won't be disappointed."

"What the fuck do you know about my disappointment? I'm *always* disappointed. Every goddamn morning when I wake up, every second my eyes are open. Sitting here talking to you right now. *Disappointed.* But, hell, I've gone everywhere in this world, tried everything to find my answer, so I may as well give you a turn. What's one more chance to win the brass ring in a long line of cons and failures? So, when can we start?"

Show him your fists! Show him! Show him NOW!

Stradley's grin widened into a smile that showed his teeth. He rose from his chair. Without so much as a moment's warning, he punched Nelson square in the face.

The old man's nose crumpled under Stradley's knuckles. His head snapped back. Blood gushed from his nostrils. The briefcase spilled from his lap, disgorging money onto the floor. Nelson slumped sideways in his chair, grabbing the armrests to stop himself from sliding out of it. He gasped for breath and gaped at Stradley—who punched him again, pummeling his head back against the chair.

"We can start right now, Mr. Nelson."

Onlookers rushed in, grabbed up the envelope and bundles of cash. Some tried to stuff it back in the briefcase while others ran off with handfuls of money. In moments, they carried it all out of sight. Nelson righted himself. Blood stained his fine clothing, and tears poured from his eyes. He trembled. Then he laughed, deep, hearty, directed at himself. In that moment, Stradley saw into Nelson's soul, saw him for an old, frail, needy man, shaking, a man on the threshold of a new world slamming the door after him on the one he left behind.

Let's show him everything he ever wanted to see. Let's take from him everything we need to set the world right. But before you show him heaven, show him your fists.

"Set the world right," Stradley muttered as he tensed his arm to throw another punch.

As Stradley's fist sped toward his face yet again, Nelson croaked, "Start right now, yes, yes, good, why... wait?" Then he laughed until Stradley's knuckles crushed his lips against his teeth.

TWO

Indeed, what Stradley had to show in the Garden did not disappoint.

Nelson regained his senses several hours later and discovered himself lying in a fetal ball on the damp earth, dressed only in his underclothes. His tremors, uncontrollable as he came alert, diminished as he gained some control of himself.

Screaming voices had dragged him awake from the recesses to which Stradley's beating had banished him. Now firelight stabbed at his eyes. He cupped a hand over them for shade and tried to make sense of what he saw. Black bars cut his view. He lay in a cage sunken a few feet into the ground on a gently sloping hill above the center of what Stradley had named his Garden. A low wall of earth surrounded half the cage, but the front portion remained clear, providing Nelson with an unobscured view down the slope to where a mob rampaged around a behemoth bonfire that shouldered back the night. Men and women chanted, shrieked, and moaned. Some wielded short whips with which they lashed their own backs. Others crawled on hands and knees, wailing whenever someone stamped on their fingers and legs. One swung a hammer at the elbows of anyone foolish enough to approach him. None of them wore more than rags, and most wore nothing, letting bloody red streaks and smears, created by their wounds, paint their flesh. Small groups joined each other in tumultuous, wrestling masses of twisting, stretching bodies, then separated and rushed back to the melee. Now and then voices hollered, alone or in unison, "Death of the flesh to free the spirit, death of the spirit to free the flesh!"

Nelson thought at first that his mind had cracked and summoned a nightmare out of a medievalist's sketchbook. But the harsh ground beneath him and the air rich with smoke and the tang of blood persuaded him he witnessed something real. Next, he guessed that Stradley had mounted a show to intimidate or impress him, but that comfort soon fled too. The wounds looked too real, and some of the bodies hit the ground in awkward, uncomfortable positions and didn't get up again. Finally, he accepted what his aged eyes showed him. Acceptance brought him no more understanding than his fantasy explanations had. The tableau weighed him down with the all-too-familiar weight of unfulfilled hopes. He had seen such things before, mad rushes to pleasures and torments of the flesh, witnessed them in many forms in many places around the world. Yet no matter what meaning people gave them these acts never penetrated more than skin deep.

I'm back on the damn bumper cars, he thought.

Then he wept, fulsome disappointment overwhelming him.

Soon a crimson glow caught his eye and drew his gaze higher.

He might rationalize and dismiss the feral orgy that unfolded around the fire, but he could not process how Stradley floated above it and looked down upon the violent ecstasy.

Beatific, in a horrible way, and limned with red light, Stradley levitated.

Twenty, thirty feet off the ground.

A hovering angel of madness.

A monster.

A man with power Nelson had never witnessed but only dreamt he might one day touch.

Now it lay within his reach. He sensed it through the space between them like the rolling concussion of a distant explosion, the air tainted by a battery-acid sharpness.

The old man scurried back until he pressed against the bars on the far side of his cage. He curled down onto himself, wrapped his arms around his knees, and wished for warmth.

As if answering a prayer, Stradley's glimmering and teary red eyes opened and flashed in his direction. A splinter of fire rushed at Nelson.

It grew until its light filled his vision, then his mind. Heat flooded him, burning off some part of him from the inside out, consuming his disappointment, carrying it away, leaving only troubled awe. Then he succumbed again to the depths of insensibility, the yawning darkness on the far side of consciousness, which he now knew Stradley himself ruled.

THREE

Beyond the bars of Nelson's cage, Stradley's acolytes worked to clear the debris left by the last night's ritual. They dragged the bodies of a man and a woman out of sight behind one of the sheds. What they did with them after that, Nelson didn't know. He watched people drift out from huts and sheds into the circle at the heart of Stradley's Garden, the ring of the bonfire pit. Judging by the height of the sun, he'd slept into early afternoon, a restless, sweaty slumber in the open brightness that had left his skin reddened and sore.

So calm in the light, so ordinary and meek, dressed in everyday clothes as if doing yard work, people set about preparing the grounds, Nelson guessed, for another night of perversions and wonders. He grasped now what Stradley held over them. The vicious guru promised his followers a way through the corrupted flesh to the pure spirit, to raw power. Judging by their unmistakable ecstasy the night before, he certainly seemed to deliver. Like Pentecostalists speaking in tongues or voodoo faithful ridden by the Loa. Yet feral, suffused with unbridled energy, and awash in blood that most ordinary people of faith preferred remain symbolic.

Not so here where the literal ruin of the flesh reigned.

A woman roused in a sunken cage neighboring Nelson's, one of a dozen or more around the Garden. She dragged herself upright. Her naked chest heaved as she coughed and then spat out bloody phlegm. Scars laced her body. Graying hair sprang from her scalp in matted tendrils that formed a dirty halo. How long had she been here, Nelson wondered. What sacrileges and miracles had she witnessed?

The woman rubbed her eyes, and then, noticing Nelson's gaze, glared at him. He looked away when she stepped out of sight behind the ground cupping the rear of her cage.

A process. Preparation and contemplation. Mortification of the flesh. Destruction of self-consciousness. Severing one's earthbound connection to free one's spirit. Exposure of one's awareness to peer behind reality's curtain and observe the truth. These things Nelson had sought for so long, only to find unfulfilled promises from spiritualists and sages, physicists and chemists alike. They all promised miracles but delivered only sleights of hand.

"What did it get me?" Nelson's voice cracked with dryness. "*Fuck all*, that's what."

"That's all anyone gets," the woman in the next cage said.

She stood at the side nearest Nelson, still half-hidden by the earth, her arms through the bars, idly scratching at the dirt. Several broken teeth rendered her smile reptilian.

Nelson pressed against his cage and reached through the bars. His fingertips came within six inches of the woman's. She flicked a pebble at him, and it bounced off the back of his hand.

"When 'fuck all' is all you got, Mr. Stradley offers real answers."

"He's a huckster like the rest. Carnival barker. Pay your money, ride the wheel. Whee!"

"They all are, though, aren't they? You trust anyone outside this place, they only fill you up with lies. Play their game to get their prizes, right? Church, the cops, the doctors, my parents. They all lied to me about who I am and where I belong in this damn world. My husband was the worst." The woman showed Nelson the underside of her forearm, dotted with small round burn scars amidst crisscrosses of long, thin keloids; it resembled a tic-tac-toe game. "See that?"

"Your husband did that to you?"

"The cigarette burns, yeah. Woke me up that way when I overslept or just for shits and giggles. The other scars? Whenever he burned me, I cut myself to mask the pain he caused with pain I created. At least I owned the hurt then. Right?" The woman pulled herself up on the bars, immodest in her nakedness, and stuck her feet through, with her shoulders pressed against the top of the cage. A mesh of scars covered her body. "Kept it up whether he burned me, cut me, beat me, or treated me like shit. Did it so long and so hard, I started to see things after I made the cuts. Thought they were hallucinations until I learned how to hurt myself so I could see what I wanted. Any time I didn't know what to do I cut myself and the answer appeared. Crazy, right? They all told me so. 'Oh, Virginia, you're off your rocker.' 'Oh, Virginia, you're going too far.' My fuckwit husband sided with them, of course. Tried to have me committed so he could shack up with a cashier from Food Wizard. That's where we met. I used to work there too. The damn checkout, me wondering who the handsome man with such good taste in beer was, looking at my future of bruises, burns, and insults, and thinking I'd found true love at last. So, we all pay our money and then ride the wheel, I guess."

Virginia hopped down from her perch.

"Why are you here?" she said.

"I want to know where we go when we die before I die."

Nelson drew his unsteady arms back into his cage. Solar heat beat down, searing and relentless. He wiped the sweat from his eyes with his quivering hands.

"We all want to know that."

"You think Stradley can show me?"

"Oh, honey, he wants to show *that* to everyone. Death of the flesh to free the spirit, death of the spirit to free the flesh."

"What does that mean?"

Virginia chuckled, exposing her rotted, fence-post teeth. Blood filled the spaces among them and pooled by her gums.

"You'll find out soon enough, sweetie."

Nelson opened his mouth to reply but coughed instead, a fit that lasted nearly a minute and culminated in him spitting out a bright, bloody gob of the rot inside his lungs.

FOUR

Night dropped around the compound like a parachute buoyed on the bonfire thermals.

People crept from the sheds and huts, came from the wild dark of the grounds, and from the farmhouse. So many more people than last night or at least more than Nelson had realized were there in his rattled state of mind. Certainly, more than Nelson expected a man like Stradley to attract, but when Stradley arrived for the revelry, even Nelson felt the tug of his native magnetism. Unavoidable. Irresistible. Charisma that devoured the self, shredded the individual will, and left only the many—and Stradley.

Firelight painted the man red at the center of the compound. His sweating skin glistened with the flickering. His bare torso displayed bruises, scars, and layers of wounds, a testament legible to those who shared its language. As he roamed among his congregation, he touched each one he passed on the forehead. Each, in turn, quivered and lit up with joy, then one by one they leapt into a brewing revelry. Soon a line of people danced a circle around the edge of the fire. Singing broke out. It calmed Nelson's shakes for a moment even as it chilled him to his core.

"Death of the flesh to free the spirit, death of the spirit to free the flesh," many sang.

Stradley approached Nelson's cage. The old man's heart leapt with unexpected hope. For mercy and relief, for an end to suffering. Despite the warmth in the air, a chill had settled deep in his old, ill bones, and his stomach raged for nourishment, his throat for water. Every motion sent waves of vertigo through his head and flocks of black bubbles across his vision. His chest ached. His skin throbbed with sunburn. His body trembled. He stayed upright by leaning on the bars of his cage. Stradley could release him from his torment. He possessed the power.

If only he unlocked the cage.

Let him out. Fed him. Clothed him.

Showed the barest touch of mercy.

Instead, Stradley passed him by and went to Virginia's cage.

"No," Nelson said. "Please. I want to see and be done with it."

Stradley unlocked *her* door. She grasped his helping hand and clambered out.

"Please," Nelson said.

Holding her head with his fingertips, Stradley leaned close to Virginia's face and spoke words inaudible to Nelson. They lit a fire in the scarred woman. She stamped her feet, grinned wide until Stradley released her, and then rushed downhill to the revelry. Seizing a softball-sized rock as she ran, she hurled it at the crowd. The stone struck a man on the ear. He folded to his knees with blood pouring down the side of his head and neck. Virginia leapt on him, punched him, scrabbled to undo his raggedy pants and pull them down. A group parted from the circle to surround her and her victim. They blocked Nelson's view, but through brief gaps, he witnessed Virginia, bloody mouth full of broken teeth, naked legs straddling the man as she choked him—and then the man smashed his elbow into her face. She reeled and spit out a tooth. Smiling, she threw herself at him again with her fingers raised like claws. Then the crowd blocked the view again.

Nelson heard the rest. Grunts and shrieks mingled with the crowd's cheers and gasps.

From the wider circle came chanting and singing. Somewhere Stradley laughed, unseen.

When the commotion around Virginia ended, the crowd fell back into the circle. Virginia didn't reappear. Nelson couldn't see her or the man she'd attacked, didn't know if they'd gone into one of the sheds, or joined the blur and shadows of the circle.

Stradley reappeared at the center of the ring.

A red aura outlined his figure. His eyes burned with a reflected flame.

A group followed him. Men and women carrying whips, which they cracked in the air, and iron brands, which they set to heat in the fire. Stradley gestured at a man in the crowd; one of his followers lashed his whip along the man's side. He yelped, staggered, resumed dancing, but another lash set him stumbling. When he fell, Stradley and his people set upon him and dragged him into the center of the circle where they tied him to a wooden post, his arms stretched so high, he stood on tiptoes.

"Oh, thank you, thank you, thank you," the man chanted. "Death of the flesh to free the spirit, death of the spirit to free the flesh! Bless me!"

"You are blessed, my friend," Stradley said. "You will show us the way."

"Yes, let me show the way, let me serve. Thank you!"

Stradley placed his right hand on the man's forehead. His red aura intensified.

The circle erupted in fresh fervor. The ones with whips and glowing red brands put them to work. Screams filled the night. Nelson couldn't tell those of pain from those of ecstasy.

Stradley's red light grew to encompass the man tied to the post.

Its energy crackled. It prickled across Nelson's flesh, summoned goosebumps, and set his hair on end. Power gathered in a rising wave poised to break on them all and release the torrent of an ocean of infinite malevolence. Nelson sensed it on the other side of what he saw, the spirit beyond the flesh. What awaited the dead beyond this life existed within their reach, its entry livid in the energy Stradley controlled.

Nelson dropped to his knees. His body shook so badly it blurred his vision.

Still, he saw well enough when Stradley retreated from the bound man, and two of the dancers came with long knives, sliced him open from throat to waist, then folded back his skin. An angelic expression of fulfillment came over him. He cried out, but his words drowned in the roar of the circle, and Nelson never heard them.

Stradley raised his arms and cheered. The huckster showing his ugly face.

Nelson understood then how he used that as a tool to control his followers. But past the façade, all Stradley's claims and offerings promised to provide Nelson with the long-sought truth. Even miracles, as attested by the eviscerated man, alive and blissful as his organs spilled out from him.

Nelson wept and watched through tears as Stradley levitated above the Garden.

The cut-open man lived long after he should've expired.

Stradley's red aura melded with the vibrancy of the flames, a brightness that owned the night, and rendered everything beyond dead black as if nothing at all existed outside of the reach of Stradley's power.

FIVE

"Death of the flesh to free the spirit, death of the spirit to free the flesh."

Stradley's voice came to Nelson as he trembled on the earthen floor of his cage. Sunlight baked him, sweaty and burned red despite shivering like a man dragged in from the icy cold. His eyelids split, and he cringed against the light. He saw Stradley staring down at him and then roused himself, dug his hands into the earth, and tried to push himself onto his feet.

"Look at you trying to stand when you should kneel for me. You disappointed yet, Mr. Nelson?" Stradley said.

"Can't say it hasn't been...," A coughing fit interrupted the old man at the end of which he gagged out a spray of blood. "...hasn't been a wild ride."

Stradley leaned forward on a walking stick. "Better than bumper cars?"

"Fucking bumper cars, fucking amusement parks is all there was, every place I looked, the same heartbreaking songs and dances, but here..." Nelson seemed at a loss.

"Here it's real. You've tasted what I can provide those who join me."

Nelson nodded.

"Want to see some more?"

Lifting his head, the old man met Stradley's confident stare. Nelson recalled himself sixty years younger and full of the youthful self-assurance and entitlement that had set him on the path to incredible wealth. He had believed then that money bought all things only to learn as he aged and saw the end of his life on the horizon that it didn't buy the things he truly wanted, things that Stradley possessed. Seemed, in fact, to have pulled out of thin air. Nelson wanted to know how.

"You've already got my nickel. Show me the rest of the damn freak show."

"Good." Stradley produced a key with which he unlocked Nelson's cage. He helped him up and out and then led him, limping, to the rim of the massive firepit. "What do you see around you?"

Nelson surveyed the sheds and huts, the tools of torture abandoned on the ground, the ashes of the bonfire, and the countless muddled footprints in the dirt and matted grass. They looked different here than from his cage. Momentous yet ephemeral, a contradiction he couldn't explain, as if they only marked the surface of something subterranean and each held within it the key to a hidden door. The little buildings shifted in his bleary eyes. They became eyeless heads with doors for mouths from which dark power overflowed. The ashes looked like a pool of milky bone powder into which he could dive and never stop sinking.

"I don't know how to describe what I see," Nelson said.

"Excellent. When you see only things you know, you gain nothing new." Stradley offered him the walking stick. "Here. You'll need this. You don't deserve it, but you'll need it."

Nelson accepted it. "Okay."

"The power wants me to break your teeth off at the gums and shove them down your throat. It wants me to yank your hair out at the roots. Right now. But I know you're not ready. Suffering has to come in the right measure and sequence."

"The power wants you to... do things?"

"Oh, yes, the power has a voice, and I've heard it all my life. When I finally listened to it, I saw so many things I couldn't describe. I found it placed the world at my feet. Come with me."

They departed the bonfire circle, the huts and sheds, and walked into the overgrown wild of the fallow farmland. Rough tracks cut through the worst of the foliage, but vines grew across their path, and branches clutched and scratched at them. Nelson strode with hesitant steps, head down, eyes focused on each next one. When he looked around, he saw an unrecognizable world full of abysses and lacuna, of flowing black lines like oil streaking the air, of gray-and-red specks that darted and swarmed like insects. He kept his eyes on his feet. The walking stick kept him steady. Every fifty yards or so, Stradley stopped and waited for him to catch up. When he heard sobbing from the trees ahead of them, Nelson planted the walking stick and raised his head.

"Someone's crying," he said.

"Isn't there always?" Stradley said.

"Who is it?"

"One of the people I want you to meet. Come on."

They rounded the curve of the track and entered a grove of Southern Live Oaks, old trees with massive roots rippling in the ground. Strung from their high branches hung another type of cage. Giant birdcages. Of the ten within sight, seven contained people. The sobbing rose from one of them, a man who looked as if he hadn't eaten in weeks. He pulled tufts of hair from his head as he wept.

Stradley approached him.

"Take comfort, brother," he said. "Death of the flesh to free the spirit, death of the spirit to free the flesh."

Stradley's voice livened the man, but he managed to say only, "Death to... the flesh...," before he collapsed back into sobbing.

The other caged people stared at Nelson with unyielding eyes, unashamed of their naked, filthy bodies, arms and legs dangling through the bars, their skin rich with bruises, cuts, and the red welts of insect bites. A stench hovered in the grove's air, rising from bodily wastes expelled onto the ground. Through his skewed perceptions, Nelson watched lines of orange insects he feared did not exist crawl on the cages and their prisoners, on the tree, on the ground. The cages appeared to stretch and drip pieces of themselves in the breeze.

"You're a torturer," Nelson said.

"No. I didn't put these people here, and I take no joy in their misery. They asked for this. I have a list thirty long of others who want the same thing, but I don't allow it if they're not ready. That's what matters. Preparing the flesh and refining the spirit. In that, I find joy. What they become when they emerge from the cage, transformed and opened to my gifts." Stradley seized the walking stick from Nelson, who lurched to keep his balance. He banged on the cages with it. "Hello! Is anyone here against their will? Would anyone like to be set free? Say the word. I'll lower your cage and let you out right now."

No one answered. They only stared at Nelson, the interloper, the doubter.

Stradley returned the cane to him, and they continued along the track. Next, they passed a place where people buried to their necks glared up at them from the ground. In another grove, people tied to the trunks of wide trees struggled to lift their heads, one on either side of a trunk, ropes digging into flesh, arms stretched around the circumference, fingers within a hair's breadth of touching. A third held several of Stradley's followers in stocks, and the fourth led to the door of a long outbuilding, like a small hangar. Nelson viewed it all through his damaged eyes, the world alive and swirling like skies in an impressionist painting, but ugly, threatening.

"All of them?" he said while Stradley unlocked the door.

"What's that?"

"All of them? Do that willingly?"

"They beg me for it once they understand what I offer. You must be ready in both flesh and spirit, or you might wind up, well, *disappointed*."

"What if I asked? Am I ready?"

Stradley considered the question. He stepped back from Nelson and gauged the frail man. A trickle of blood ran from the corner of Nelson's lips. He hadn't even noticed it. Only the walking stick kept him vertical.

"You needy bastard, who do you think you are? The power tells me to beat you deaf just for asking," Stradley said. "But I know better. You asked me that very question just by coming here, and, Mr. Nelson, you are so close to ready. All the pieces are there awaiting your full understanding to shuffle them into place." Stradley opened the door and ushered Nelson into the building. "Once you have that, then I can show you what you want to see."

They passed through a small anteroom and then into a large storage area full of weapons. Rows of racks and shelves held a motley collection of handguns, rifles, machetes, clubs, land mines, grenades, knives, and other mechanisms of killing. Stradley guided him through the room to the far end without comment. The contents of the room conveyed everything that needed saying. This was a stockpile of death awaiting delivery.

They came to another door and stepped into a side chamber.

A cube made of plastic sheeting—a room within a room—occupied the central space. Wires and tubes connected it to various machines and a ventilation system.

Two men and two women sat inside on folding chairs around a card table. They wore t-shirts, shorts, and jeans, and looked healthier and better healed than most of Stradley's other followers.

"I arranged this for you," Stradley said.

"Another sideshow," Nelson said. "You're wasting my time."

"You'll change your mind soon enough. Watch."

Stradley moved close to the sheeting. The four within gathered near him on the other side.

"Do any of you want out? Changed your mind? Reconsidered? You know I'll open the seal right now if you do."

The four shook their heads.

"Did I force any of you in here? Coerce you? Intimidate you?" Stradley pointed at the old man. "It's important that Mr. Nelson understands what he's seeing."

Again, the four shook their heads.

"Good, very good. We drew lots, didn't we? Because so many people volunteered for this." The woman nodded. "Excellent. Marybeth, please show us the container then proceed."

Inside the cube, Marybeth raised a steel container roughly the size of a thermos, waited several seconds while Nelson took a good look, and then set it on the table. She unscrewed the cap and set it beside it. Producing a new top with a nozzle, she screwed it onto the canister. Once it locked into position, she put the cylinder on the floor at the cube's center and then depressed a button on its side.

"Expensive stuff you're about to see in action. This one cost $15,000 alone," Stradley said. "You wouldn't believe how hard it is to find people selling, but they're out there, oh, yes, and money sure does grease those wheels."

A gray mist plumed from the nozzle and spread within the cube.

An instant later, the men and women inside crumpled to the floor. The spray continued for several seconds and rendered the interior of the cube invisible. To Nelson's eyes, it looked alive, writhing to free itself from its meager cell, hungry to touch him. In minutes it dissipated. The four lay dead where they had fallen, eyes rolled back in their sockets, blood dribbling from their nostrils and lips, their skin pale.

Nelson staggered a step and used the walking stick to regain stability. "Why? Why did they kill themselves like that? Why did you ask them to do that?"

"So you would understand what the fortune you're going leave me will buy. They had no fear. You understand? They knew what you wish to know. Now, Mr. Nelson, if I ask *you* if you are ready, what will your answer be?"

SIX

Yes.

Of course, Nelson said yes.

With no real idea of his true readiness, he accepted whatever Stradley guided him to next. He hadn't paid his money to *not* take the ride, and despite the vileness of what Stradley had so far showed him, here he had seen more faith, witnessed more real power, and felt closer to the edge of the answers he desired than anywhere else he'd ever sought them.

The rest unfolded over several days. Stradley stayed with him through most of it.

They began with diluted poison mixed into fine scotch, a celebratory concession. The alcohol burned Nelson's throat, and the poison gnawed at his guts.

Next, he entered one of the tree cages and found it much worse than his first prison. He emerged three days later, dehydrated and confused.

His disorientation pleased Stradley, who spoke of breaking down barriers, killing the flesh until only the spirit remained and then killing the spirit until only the truth endured.

Two days buried up to his neck. Four tied to a Live Oak.

With every passing second, the world became a stranger and less certain place for Nelson until, in the end, he almost believed he had left it behind. Or that it had never existed. A dream of life, of being, from which he now awakened. Everywhere he looked, he saw strange shapes and colors, an infestation of unreality.

By the time Stradley and four of his followers brought him into the armory, Nelson couldn't walk on his own. His tremors rocked him. He ached for food and drink. Open wounds and sores riddled his sunburned, peeling flesh, and his limbs screamed with itching insect bites. They took him past the weapons to the back room. The plastic sheeting cube and the equipment that had maintained it lay piled in a corner. Eight gurneys occupied that space now, all but one of them bearing a motionless human figure under a dirty black sheet. On the one empty gurney, a folded black sheet waited at the foot.

Against one wall, a standing mirror reflected the overhead fluorescents and gave the light a hazy quality.

In a corner of the room stood two chairs and a card table, a manila envelope upon it.

Two of the entourage helped seat Nelson at the table, while the other two waited by the empty gurney. The old man eyed the envelope as Stradley took the other seat.

"What are these?" Nelson's hoarse voice barely broke a whisper.

"Don't you recall?" Stradley opened the envelope and slid out several pages printed with small words. Colorful sticky tags prodded out from some of the papers. "They're contracts and releases you promised to sign if I showed you where we go when we die. They leave all of your earthly fortune to me."

Nelson nodded, a gesture difficult to discern, considering how much his head bobbed. "I remember, but you just dragged me through the freak show. I'm waiting for the main attraction."

With a smirk, Stradley said, "It's going to begin once you sign the papers. Unorthodox of me, I understand, to ask you to keep your end of our bargain before I've kept mine, but, trust me, you won't be in any frame of mind to do this after you see the show. It's the only way we can keep our deal."

"What if you're tricking me?"

Stradley said nothing for several seconds. His red aura appeared, painting his person with a cold, ruby light. He lifted from his chair, rose several feet in the air, and regarded Nelson like a parent regards a doubtful child.

"Have I not shown you miracles enough to earn your trust?" he said. "I have but one mystery left to share."

"Yes, yes." Nelson pawed at the pen until he snagged it in quaking, arthritic fingers. He sifted through one page after another, signing where the sticky tags indicated until no papers remained. One of Stradley's people gathered the signed documents, looked them over, and gave a sharp nod of confirmation.

"You've done all of humanity a tremendous favor. Your resources will allow me to tear away the veil of falsehoods under which we suffer and show everyone what the universe really is and how awful our place in it is. Right now, humanity still thinks the world is a place for the living. They go on about their lives, worried about surviving and thriving, arguing over the right way, the best way, their favorite way to live, and they think killing one another is the greatest of sins. I'm going to show them all how wrong they are and teach them death is the way. Death of the flesh to free the spirit, death of the spirit to free the flesh."

Two of Stradley's people helped Nelson from his chair and over to the empty gurney, where the other two helped him onto it.

Stradley wheeled one of the other gurneys into place beside Nelson's and peeled back the black sheet. Virginia lay there, dead, discolored, and yet better preserved than Nelson expected for a days-old corpse.

"Are you ready to see, Mr. Nelson?" Stradley said.

Without shifting his gaze away from Virginia, Nelson said, "*Am* I ready?"

"Yes, I think you are."

He cupped a hand over Nelson's mouth, pinched the old man's nose shut with the other, and waited. Nelson jerked, tried to bat Stradley's hands away, but his body possessed so little life after all his tribulations, and tremors robbed him of his strength. Seconds became a minute, then minutes, and then a gray fog overcame Nelson's vision, darkened to black, and he died.

SEVEN

Nelson's eyes popped open.

The world dizzied him.

The room, the gurneys, the dismantled cube, the table and chairs, Stradley's people—it all looked as if it had sprung to life from a cubist painting. He saw the world as if cracked in two and pieces pressed together misaligned. He looked at the backs of Stradley's people with one eye and the fronts from another, both still part of his gaze. The disorientation should've nauseated him, but he felt nothing more than the light stinging his eyes as they adjusted.

The view tilted. He moved around the room, but not under his control.

He glimpsed the gurneys, on which the dead figures now sat up, black sheets peeled back, bodies wrinkled and spotted with rot. He recognized two of the dead from his first night caged in the Garden, the mystery of what happened to them now solved. He knew the other four from the makeshift gas chamber, Marybeth and the volunteers who died to show him what his wealth would permit Stradley to unleash on the world.

The scene lurched again.

Nelson felt none of it, only saw it.

He felt nothing at all beyond the grasp of his eyes.

A terrifying silence surrounded him.

The mirror gleamed.

One line of his sight approached it. From the other, he saw the back of Virginia's naked corpse shuffling toward the glass. He recognized her crisscross scars and cigarette burns. Then one of his eyes found the reflection, and he stared at himself while the other watched Virginia sway in front of the mirror. Long seconds passed before Nelson made sense of what he saw.

The single eye staring into the mirror looked upon itself, peering out from folds of skin at Virginia's waist above her right leg. Someone turned Virginia to face a second standing corpse, and Nelson met the gaze of his second eye staring out from the dead flesh of a man he had watched die. His two eyes regarded each other. The rotted skin around them blinked.

Nelson wished to scream, but he had no lungs, no throat, no voice. He wished to run but found no footing. He wished to die—and then understood: He already had. Stradley had killed him then resurrected him to show him what he had so long desired. *Where do we go when we die?* The main attraction unfolded within Stradley's secret big top. More eyes peered from the other corpses in the room. All stark with confusion and shock. None able to communicate even with the flesh they inhabited. Only passengers now, their life's energy imparted to dead flesh, reallocated and... preserved?

How long would this last? Was this the eternal afterlife?

Nelson's view whirled again as someone forced Virginia to sit. Stradley sat across from him, smiling, looking him right in the eye. At the same time, his other eye focused on him from across the room. Stradley's gaunt face resembled a skull.

No, Nelson thought. *Not eternal life.*

Death. He is death.

Eternal death.

THE DISTANCE TO LOHATCHIE

The Dead in Their Masses—unlike some of the other Corpse Fauna stories—enjoyed a fairly straightforward path to publication. It was a story I wanted to tell as soon as I finished "The Dead Bear Witness" so when Vince Sneed asked me to contribute to a new anthology of zombie stories he was editing to follow up *The Dead Walk*, I knew the time had come to write it. I picked up only a short time after Cornell, Della, and Mason break out of prison and chronicled their attempt to journey to Lohatchie. In retrospect, I went a little easy on them for the first leg of their trip, so their lives only got harder when I revised the story for this new edition. Regardless, Vince was pleased with the original version and included it in *The Dead Walk Again*, published by Padwolf Publishing in 2007 with a cover painted by Steve Blickenstaff.

The threads of the overarching Corpse Fauna cycle really start coming together here. Cornell and Della strengthen their relationship. Cornell meets Birch. And then he meets the Red Man, a dark counterweight to St. Bianco from *Tears of Blood*. Before this Cornell thought he was only struggling to stay alive and find a safe place to live—but after his encounter with Darrell Philip Stradley, he is made into something more. A man with a role to play in something greater than himself. And that's not something that sits well with someone whose entire existence has been a stick poked in the eye of authority.

I revisited some of the themes from *The Dead Bear Witness*. Cornell's unease being part of society. His resentment of authority both spiritual and worldly. His sense that a terrible fate awaits him sometime in the future. But also his need—despite what he believes about himself—to not be alone. In a world overrun by the living dead, most people would see Camp Cady as luxurious sanctuary, but Cornell sees it for what it really is: a comfortable trap. That's all life can ever be unless you're making your own rules. But how does an outlaw define himself in a world where there are no longer any laws? Cornell may be a robber, but he's no savage, and in many cases, he proves the better of those who represent any kind of authority. His friendship with Birch reflects Vale's experiences from *Tears of Blood*. No matter how weird he thinks it is, Birch lives in the world as it is not as he wants it to be—at least as far as he understands it. Keep up or fall behind. Adapt or die. Or be damned to a living death. Trying to understand a new world isn't easy, but the ones who make the attempt are the ones who matter most.

When I began work on *The Dead in Their Masses*, I intended it to conclude Cornell's story. It wouldn't have been the end of Corpse Fauna, but it would've brought everything in Cornell's piece of it full circle and shown how things turned out for him. As I wrote it, though, I realized there was much more to Cornell and his role in the dead world than I could cover in this one story. Then I began to wonder what might happen if Cornell and Vale should meet, and *The Dead in Their Masses* turned out to be the only next major chapter in the Cornell's story, not the last.

Around the time *The Dead Walk Again* was published, Vince and I talked plans for a Corpse Fauna collection, a thick volume collecting all the published material, some new short pieces, and the last big chapter of Cornell's story, all to be published by Die Monster Die. It would pick up from where *The Dead in Their Masses* left off and it would answer all the open questions and explain many of the secrets of the walking dead. We were excited. I started writing. Vince was looking forward to designing the book and creating the cover. As sometimes happens, though, the real world derailed our plans. When Dark Quest Books revived Corpse Fauna, this volume stood ready to go. We made it as far as Glen Ostrander's gruesomely stunning cover, which, thankfully, adorns this edition before those plans also collided with unpleasant realities and derailed.

Twelve years later, Corpse Fauna returns from the dead once more.

James Chambers
September 2019

ABOUT THE AUTHOR

James Chambers is an award-winning author of horror, crime, fantasy, and science fiction. He wrote the Bram Stoker Award®-winning graphic novel, *Kolchak the Night Stalker: The Forgotten Lore of Edgar Allan Poe* and was nominated for a Bram Stoker Award for his story, "A Song Left Behind in the Aztakea Hills." *Publisher's Weekly* gave his collection of four Lovecraftian-inspired novellas, *The Engines of Sacrifice*, a starred review and described it as "...chillingly evocative."

He is the author of the short story collections *On the Night Border* and *Resurrection House* and several novellas, including *The Dead Bear Witness*, *Tears of Blood*, and *The Dead in Their Masses*, in the Corpse Fauna novella series, and the dark urban fantasy, *Three Chords of Chaos*.

His short stories have been published in numerous anthologies, including *After Punk: Steampowered Tales of the Afterlife*, *The Best of Bad-Ass Faeries*, *The Best of Defending the Future*, *Chiral Mad 2*, *Chiral Mad 4*, *Deep Cuts*, *Dragon's Lure*, *Fantastic Futures 13*, *Footprints in the Stars*, *Gaslight and Grimm*, *The Green Hornet Chronicles*, *Hardboiled Cthulhu*, *Heroes of the Realm*, *In An Iron Cage*, *In Harm's Way*, *Kolchak the Night Stalker: Passages of the Macabre*, *The Pulp Horror Book of Pho-*

bias, Qualia Nous, Shadows Over Main Street (1 and 2), *The Spider: Extreme Prejudice, To Hell in a Fast Car, Truth or Dare, TV Gods, Walrus Tales, Weird Trails*; the chapbook *Mooncat Jack*; and the magazines *Bare Bone, Cthulhu Sex*, and *Allen K's Inhuman*.

He co-edited the anthology, *A New York State of Fright: Horror Stories from the Empire State*, which received a Bram Stoker Award nomination.

He has also written and edited numerous comic books including *Leonard Nimoy's Primortals*, the critically acclaimed "The Revenant" in *Shadow House*, and *The Midnight Hour* with Jason Whitley.

He is a member of the Horror Writers Association and recipient of the 2012 Richard Laymon Award and the 2016 Silver Hammer Award.

He lives in New York.

Visit his website: www.jameschambersonline.com.

ABOUT THE ARTISTS

Glen Ostrander (cover) is a Freelance Artist and Illustrator who has created artwork in the fantasy/horror genre for a wide variety of commercial clients. He is known for his evocative work and continues to bring his creations to life by finding daily inspiration near his home, in the wild mountains of New Hampshire, where he lives with his wonderful wife Anna, his devilish dog Jojo, and his fiendish feline Floyd.

Jason Whitley (interior) is the illustrator and co-creator of *The Midnight Hour*. Jason's work as a newspaper illustrator has appeared across the country and won many awards. His portrait of civil rights leader Charlotte Hawkins Brown is in the Charlotte Hawkins Brown Museum. With writer Scott Eckelaert, he co-created and illustrated the classic comic-strip, *Sea Urchins. Sea Urchins* has been collected into four volumes. The fourth volume, So Long, Frozen Ocean will be released in 2020. Jason leads a Hermes and Telly Award-winning multimedia team of five in North Carolina. He's working on a crime-noir graphic novel with no set release date and looking forward to the complete *The Midnight Hour* collection from eSpec Books in 2020.